The Anglo-Indian Way

Errol O'Brien grew up in Kolkata. He worked in the tea industry and retired as chief tea taster and buyer of the Tea Trading Corporation of India. He has been an active quizzer and quizmaster. He has also coached students in public speaking. His articles on tea have been published in the *Statesman* and he wrote a column for the *Telegraph*, Kolkata. He has written two books: *The Tree of Knowledge* and *Amar Calcutta, My Kolkata*.

THE

Anglo-Indian

WAY

Celebrating the Lives
of the Anglo-Indians of India

edited by ERROL O'BRIEN

RUPA

Published by
Rupa Publications India Pvt. Ltd. 2013
7/16, Ansari Road, Daryaganj
New Delhi 110002

Sales centres:
Allahabad Bengaluru Chennai
Hyderabad Jaipur Kathmandu
Kolkata Mumbai

ISBN: 978-81-291-2108-0

10 9 8 7 6 5 4 3 2 1

Typeset in Minion Pro 11/14.5

Printed at Repro Knowledgecast Limited, Thane

To my late parents, Eric and Edith.
And to my grandchildren,
so that they remember their roots.

Contents

Introduction

What does 'The Anglo-Indian Way' mean? The title of this book borrows from the inspirational and recently released anthem of the Anglo-Indian community in India, the lyrics of which are included in the following pages.

'The Anglo-Indian Way' is a way of life—an outlook that is about being proud of one's roots and heritage while not being afraid of integrating with the larger society. I have chosen to show this through chronicles of men and women and entire families who have lived their lives in this way. Theirs are accomplished lives, and they have become symbols of pride and models of virtue and skill for both their community and their country. By no means are they the only Anglo-Indians worth celebrating; there are so many men and women of the community whose heroic lives have gone unsung and unrecorded, that it will take several volumes to do justice to them. My selection is inherently incomplete; it was constrained by time and space.

I am deeply grateful to my fellow contributors—Derek

O'Brien, Andy O'Brien, Ashok Malik, Andrew Scolt and Peter Moore—for writing about personalities who they have either known or whose lives they have seen at close quarters. Their contributions bring added depth and warmth to this anthology. Other writers such as Ruskin Bond, Soutik Biswas and Ronald Forbes have kindly consented to having their previously published articles reproduced here, for which I am grateful.

I have arranged these narratives chronologically, in order to give the reader a sense of how time, and the changing challenges and opportunities it brings, has impacted the Anglo-Indian community.

Excluded from *The Anglo-Indian Way* are profiles of illustrious members of the Anglo-Indian diaspora, now spread across continents and deserving of a book in themselves. My purpose was to pay tribute to those Anglo-Indians who have stayed on in the country of their birth and origin and made their mark here. This is their story.

Errol O'Brien

The Anglo-Indian Way

Vande mataram vande mataram
Sujalam sufalam malayaja shitalam
Proud of our roots
Proud of right now
Proud of our tomorrow
We'll show them how
Take a challenge on
We must stay strong
Live each day
So let's together say
It's the greatness
of the Anglo-Indian way
Shasyashyamalam, mataram!

—Anthem paying tribute to the Anglo-Indian community from Derek O'Brien & Associates
(The anthem can be viewed on this link: https://www.youtube.com/watch?v=hiBoC8bNAWs)

SIKANDAR SAHIB

James Skinner (1778–1841)

James Skinner's life was an exotic blend of the East and the West. An adventurer, a mercenary and a legendary soldier, his name is inextricably linked with the military history of India. The amalgamation of cultures that characterized the lives of the earliest Anglo-Indians was exemplified in his life story—one that combined the haze of hookah smoke with the revelry of the British army.

James Skinner was born in Kolkata to a Scottish father, Lieutenant-Colonel Hercules Skinner, who was serving as an officer in the East India Company. His mother was a Rajput. At the age of fourteen she had been abducted by Hercules Skinner while he was an ensign. She lived with him and eventually they married. They had six children, three boys and three girls.

The meeting of the East and West in the Skinner household was not a happy one. Hercules was keen on a European upbringing for his children, including the girls. His wife, however, wanted the girls to be brought up in traditional

Rajput fashion. Unable to resolve this difference with her husband, and unwilling to accept the Western influence on her daughters, Mrs Skinner finally took her own life. James, at the time, was twelve.

He was educated at an English school in Kolkata and then at a boarding school. His father apprenticed him later to a printing firm and again to a law organization. Neither of these appealed to him, as his wandering spirit was yearning for a life of warfare and adventure.

James Skinner wanted to join the private army of the East India Company but was denied a commission simply because he was of mixed parentage: an Anglo-Indian. Undeterred, he looked for employment in his chosen profession elsewhere, and finally, at the age of sixteen, found a place in the Maratha Army where he was drafted as an ensign. Here he served under Benoit de Boigne, the Supreme Commander of Maharaja Scindia's army at Gwalior. Boigne took to the young lad who showed much promise as a soldier. Boigne was also no less impressed by his family lineage, as the Skinners had at one time distinguished themselves in the service of William the Conqueror of England, in the eleventh century. Skinner's skills as a soldier were honed under Boigne's leadership and he remained in the Scindia army for eight years.

In 1800, at the Battle of Uniara, Skinner was shot in the groin and left for dead on the battlefield. He fought for his life and managed to survive for two days without food or water. In his most desperate moments he prayed for help, resolving to build a church if his prayers were answered. Finally, he was saved by a cobbler's wife, who was searching for valuables left on the bodies of the dead in the battlefield. She found him half dead, took him in and nursed him back to health in the enemy camp. Later, he rewarded the woman and regarded her as his mother.

He could fulfill his promise of building a church many years after this, when the St James' Church was erected by him in Delhi. It came up between 1826 and 1836 and was consecrated in 1836. It's a grand building, and is considered to be the oldest church in Delhi. At the time, he spent Rs 95,000 in building it.

Back in 1803, the outbreak of the Anglo-Maratha Wars led to all Anglo-Indians being dismissed from service from the Maratha armies. So Skinner lost his job despite his loyalty to the Scindias. The British forces under Lord Lake defeated the Scindias and about 800 men who served with the Scindias offered to join the victors. When asked who they would like to have as a leader, they declared in unison, 'Sikandar Sahib'. Thus was formed, on 23 February 1803, at Hansi, in what is now Haryana, one of the finest fighting units in the Indian cavalry.

There followed a period of continuous warfare for this Irregular Cavalry Corps, and by 1814 it grew into the first, second and third regiments of Skinner's Horse, each with a strength of a thousand men. Word of Skinner's exploits reached Buckingham Palace and King George IV conferred on him the rank of Lieutenant-Colonel in 1828. Skinner's Horse was completely incorporated into the British Indian Army only in 1861, when it was named the First Regiment of Bengal Cavalry.

Skinner's Horse was also known as the Yellow Boys because of their colourful uniform, one of the most distinctive of the armies of the time. Mindful of his Rajput heritage, Skinner had decreed that his men would tie a yellow saffron cloth around their heads when they went into battle. The 'do or die' spirit of the Rajputs was ingrained in his men and they would ride off to either encounter victory or martyrdom in war. The Yellow Boys were a feared lot and James Skinner at one time was the most famous mercenary leader in north India.

For his exploits, he was rewarded by the British with a 'jagir' in Hansi, which had a yield of Rs 20,000 a year. In his manners and modes of living, Skinner was more Indian than European. He married many times, and had a large family. He had country houses in Hansi and Bilaspur, and part of his family also settled in Delhi.

He loved Indian food and smoked a hookah. He was comfortable speaking Persian, which was the court and intellectual language of the day. He was the author of *Kitab-I-Tasrih-al-Aqvam* (the History of the Origin and Distinguishing Marks of Different Castes in India) in Persian. Skinner belonged to an era when the lines between the two races—the British and the Indians—were not as firmly drawn as they were to become post the revolt of 1857. He had no inhibitions fraternizing with his staff and subordinates and in fact took pains to remember their names and the villages from which they came and even dining with them.

He died in December 1841 and was buried in the Cantonment burial ground in Delhi.

Forty days later, his body was disinterred and 200 men of the Skinner's regiments escorted his body to the St James' Church where he was laid to rest in a vault of white marble, below the altar.

In 1903, Skinner's Horse was renamed the First Duke of York's Own Lancers. The regiment was involved in major operations in the three Afghan Wars, the Sikh Wars, the Boxer Rebellion in China, and the two World Wars. In 1939, the regiment stopped using horses and a motorized unit went to

Sudan during World War II where it beat back an Italian attack.

After India's independence, the regiment became part of the Indian Army, changing its name to Skinner's Horse (1st Horse). In 1965, the unit was equipped with Sherman tanks and became armoured.

James Skinner's family lives on in India and in other parts of the world. His eldest son, who was from a Muslim wife, and his line settled in Meerut. Parts of the family are now in the UK and Australia, too.

In 1960, Lieutenant-Colonel Michael Skinner, a great-great-grandson, took command of Skinner's Horse and was the first Skinner to command the regiment since its founder's death.

In 2003, a special service was held at St James' Church to commemorate 200 years of Skinner's Horse. Thus, the legacy of this early Anglo-Indian and memories of his colourful and dramatic life remain alive in India to this day.

—Errol O'Brien

THE POET AND FREETHINKER

Henry Vivian Louis Derozio (1809–1831)

My country! In thy day of glory past
A beauteous halo circled round thy brow,
And worshipped as a deity thou wast.
Where is that glory, where that reverence now?
The eagle pinion is chained down at last,
And grovelling in the lowly dust art thou;
Thy minstrel hath no wreath to weave for thee
Save the sad story of thy misery!

—from 'To India, My Native Land'
by Henry Vivian Derozio

Henry Vivian Derozio wrote this poem at a time when the idea of nationalism—and the concept of India as a country—was still nascent. Years later, Bankim Chandra Chatterjee would give voice to this very thought in his song 'Vande Mataram' ('Hail Mother India'). But Henry Derozio, a young rebel poet born into the Anglo-Indian community of Kolkata, first articulated in verse and song the feeling of helplessness of a country brought to ruin by English imperialists. He was also one of India's earliest writers in the English language, his works foreshadowing Bankim's *Rammohan's Wife*, the first English novel written by an Indian.

Derozio is now synonymous with rebellion and patriotism, a youthful figure who inspired a whole generation of students to change their ways of thinking and the world around them. Yet, in his lifetime and even many years later, his name was vilified both by his own community and those he angered with his iconoclastic words.

A little north of St Theresa's Church in Calcutta is 155 Lower Circular Road (now A. J. C. Bose Road). It is a decrepit, uncared-for building, falling into ruin and unpainted for years. This house was once the home of this man who fought for freedom of thought, and who came as a breath of fresh air in the Eurasian community of the city. He was also perhaps one of modern India's greatest teachers.

Derozio was born in 1809 to an Indo-Portuguese father, Francis Derozio, and his British wife, Sophie Johnson, at Entally-Paddapukur in Kolkata. Records show that he was baptized at St John's Cathedral. His father worked in the firm of J. Scott and Company. Little is known of his two brothers and sisters.

At the age of eight, Derozio was enrolled at the Drummond Academy at Dharamtolla, established by David Drummond in 1810. Drummond, a Scotsman, had modelled the school on British ones. It offered the study of Grammar, English literature and Latin classics, with an English system of examination. Drummond Academy was a crucible of creativity for its students. A whole generation of men learnt how to be free from traditional ways of thinking at the academy, and books and ideas were considered the greatest weapons in fighting against orthodoxy.

Derozio proved himself a brilliant student at the school. Drummond instilled in him a yearning for knowledge and free, rational thinking. Derozio also got his first tastes of English literature, philosophy and history there. The works of Robert Burns and accounts of the French Revolution deeply influenced him and helped shape his attitudes.

Derozio left school at the age of fourteen and joined his father's commercial venture. After his father's death when he was sixteen, he moved to an indigo plantation in Bhagalpur owned by his uncle. Stirred by the scenic beauty of the Ganges and the lush countryside, and with the ripple of the river in his ears, the boy began to weave songs in his mind. He began writing poetry.

Derozio's poetry appeared in *The Indian Gazette*, run by Dr John Grant, under the pseudonym Juvenis. These lines from 'Happy Meeting' were published in March 1825:

> How keen the pang, how sad the thought,
> How oft to quiet remembrance brought,
> When friend from friend is forc'd to part
> When distance separates the heart

Dr Grant's encouragement and appreciation of his work led Derozio to publish his poetry in the form of a book.

The edition was well received and Derozio published his second volume, which was a reprint of the first, with a few notable additions. This stanza from 'Heaven' eerily foretold the famous words of Tagore from his poem 'Where the Mind Is Without Fear':

Where sighs are ne'er heard and where tears are ne'er
shed
Where hearts that might elsewhere have broken and
bled,
Where grief is unfelt, where its name is unknown
Where the music of gladness is heard in each tone
Where melody vibrates from harps of pure gold

As a poet, Derozio idolized Lord Byron and was influenced by the Romantics. 'The Fakir of Jungheera' (1828) is a long lyrical poem filled with descriptions of the region around Bhagalpur. It recounts the tale of a religious mendicant who saves the woman he once loved from committing Sati. Derozio's was one of the first Indian voices to be raised against the practice of Sati, the abolition of which would later become one of Raja Ram Mohan Roy's greatest contributions to India.

Meanwhile, in Kolkata, the Hindu College had been founded by Raja Ram Mohan Roy and others in 1817. It would later become the renowned Presidency College, one of the first centres of learning to provide a Western style of education to Indian youth. Derozio learnt that a faculty position was on offer at the college and returned to Kolkata to take up teaching at the age of seventeen.

As a teacher, Derozio was innovative and brilliant. His wide reading helped him to fill his lectures with new and radical ideas. He was more than a poet or a professor at the college. He heralded a new era in the life of the English-educated Bengali and was the spearhead of the Young Bengal movement. Although Eurasian by birth, Derozio's native Bengal fuelled his patriotic spirit and he considered himself very much an Indian—and this informed all his ideals and actions.

Derozio encouraged in his students the questioning of cultural and religious practices as well as a spirit of free expression, the yearning for knowledge and the passion to affirm their identities as Indians. This intellectual and patriotic ambition made the college the cradle of new thought and social change—embodied most flamboyantly by this newly appointed fiery young Anglo-Indian professor and poet.

Derozio's students came to be known as Derozians. He organized discussions where ideas and social norms were openly debated. He also encouraged his students to venture into journalism, to spread their ideas in a society that was on the verge of massive change. Apart from articles censuring Hindu practices, his students wrote about the emancipation of women and criticized many aspects of British rule, too A true educator, Derozio took great pleasure in interacting with his students. He was close to most in age; some of them, in fact, were older. The motto of the Derozians was: 'He who will not reason is a bigot, he who cannot reason is a fool, and he who does not reason is a slave.'

The spark lit by Derozio flared into the Young Bengal movement, whose members took part in fundamental social reforms. Some of his followers converted to Christianity and some others went on to rebel against orthodoxy and join the Brahmo Samaj, one of the most influential religious movements responsible for the making of modern India. It was conceived in Kolkata in 1830 by Debendranath Tagore and Raja Ram Mohan Roy.

The radicalism of Derozio's teachings and his student group caused an intense backlash against him. The Hindu-dominated management committee of the college, under the chairmanship of Radhankanto Deb, moved to expel him from the faculty. Derozio's efforts to defend himself proved of no avail and he was made to put in his resignation.

The anti-imperialist tone of his writings also alienated Derozio from the Anglo-Indian community, which was overwhelmingly pro-British. Derozio struck a contrary note and urged his fellow Anglo-Indians to unite and cooperate with other native inhabitants of India; he argued that it would be in their interest.

Derozio's poems reflected a 'struggle for freedom', envisioning a united, single India at a time when the country was a loose confederacy of states. The East India Company, in its efforts to establish hegemony, had by means of oppression stretched its trading rights to occupational rights. The idea of nationalism was being formulated all over the world. Its impact in India was beginning to be felt with the dawning of the Bengal Renaissance, whose chief mentor was Derozio.

Derozio was an atheist and had set aside conventional Christian (and other religious) beliefs. He encouraged the questioning of orthodox Hindu customs and tradition, basing his ideas on the conventions of the Italian Renaissance and its offshoot, Rationalism. Despite being viewed as an iconoclast, Derozio's ideas were tolerated by the English community since they were not in direct conflict with the basic tenets of Christianity and as long as he only criticized orthodox Hinduism.

Though he continued to interact with his students, Derozio's expulsion had put him in dire financial straits. He was, however, able to do more in his endeavours to encourage his students to be freethinkers even after resigning from the faculty by helping them to bring out several newspapers. His influence over them did not lessen, either then or even years after his death.

At the end of the year 1831, Derozio contracted cholera, which was at that time a fatal disease. Only twenty-two years old, he died on 26 December 1831.

Almost two centuries later, in a strange quirk of fate, the institution that expelled him chose to honour him. The Presidency College auditorium was named Derozio Hall after him, and a bust and plaque commemorating his life and work were installed. There is also a Derozio building on the campus. His grave lies at the Park Street Cemetery in Kolkata and the Anglo-Indian community meets there, in silent prayer, on his birthday every year.

Poet, radical, freethinker—many words can be used to describe the extraordinary man who lived so short a life but had such a profound effect on society and the lives of so many people. These lines from his poem 'The Poet's Grave' are perhaps the most appropriate words by which to remember the life of this remarkable man:

> There nothing o'er him but the heavens shall weep
> There never pilgrims at his shrine shall bend
> But holy stars alone their nightly vigils keep!

—ERROL O'BRIEN

A KNIGHT IN SHINING ARMOUR
Sir Henry Gidney (1873–1942)

The life of Sir Henry Gidney was a story of grandeur; his flamboyant lifestyle, the stuff of legends. He walked with the kings and princes of his day, and yet, is best remembered for his intellectual rigour and his passionate espousal of the position of Anglo-Indians within the political and social setup of newly independent India.

Gidney was born on 9 July 1873, in Igatpuri in the Western Ghats, about eighty miles from Mumbai. He finished his education in various institutions across the country, in Bangalore, Allahabad and Kolkata. At sixteen, he joined the Calcutta Medical College. He was a brilliant student and was ranked first in the final examinations. At thirty-six, he was an FRCS, a research scholar and a lecturer in ophthalmology at Oxford and a Fellow of the Royal Society.

Gidney qualified for the Indian Medical Service and joined the army, where he moved up rapidly to the rank of Lieutenant-Colonel.

Between 1898 and 1901, in China, the Boxer Uprising happened, led by the Righteous Harmony Society. The society was formed as a reaction against what was perceived as the evil influences of the West—widespread opium addiction, foreign invasions, economic hardships and the growing influence of Christianity in the country.

Gidney rendered active service as a physician during the rebellion. He performed excellently on the battlefront and was favourably mentioned in dispatches for his efforts during these encounters.

After the China sojourn, Gidney was posted as a civil surgeon at Kohima. Here, too, he lived dangerously, and once helped to stave off a Naga raid with accurate sharpshooting and bravado. Disgruntled when he was left out of the accolades accorded to others after the minor victory, he asked for a transfer.

World War I took its toll on Gidney. Posted at Peshawar in the North-West Frontier Province, he was part of the party tasked to defend Fort Shabkadar. He took a bullet and the wound finally made him seek retirement from the Indian Medical Service.

Now Gidney set up his private practice in Mumbai. The welfare of the Anglo-Indian community became one of his concerns and he started devoting much of his free time to this end. In 1937, he formed the Anglo-Indian and Domiciled European Association to highlight the problems faced by the people of his community.

Gidney and the association became closely involved in the changing political situation within the country. He represented the Anglo-Indian community at all the three Round Table Conferences in England set up to bring about constitutional reforms in India. He was also present during the visits of the Simon Commission and the Cripps Mission to India.

He was one among five delegates to speak at the Round Table Conference in London, in the presence of King George V. In his speech he made an impassioned plea on behalf of the Anglo-Indian community. He referred to the Anglo-Indians as 'my people' but then corrected himself and referred to them as 'Your Majesty's people and my community'. The corrected statement reportedly brought a smile to King George's face.

Gidney was knighted in 1931. Earlier, in 1921, after the Central Legislative Assembly was formed, he was nominated to it by the Viceroy as a representative of the community. At the Assembly, not only was he well regarded for his intellectual depth, but his well-attired persona was one of the most elegant and pleasing sights among the Indian leaders.

His brilliant oratory and ready wit made him a legend. After a particular dissertation by Mohammed Ali Jinnah, Sir Henry summarised his speech with a pithy, humorous statement: 'The Hon'ble member who has just sat down has not only got the bull by the horns but the cow by the udder end.'

The House erupted in laughter.

Sir Henry was an epicurean; he was a lover of art and vintage wine. His house on Prithviraj Road in Delhi was filled with beautiful and famous paintings, Persian carpets and chandeliers. In fact, he headed the All-India Arts and Crafts Society as well.

Amongst his friends were members of Indian royalty. Hunting trips and *shikar* were a part of the lavish lifestyle of the rich during the days of the British Raj.

In 1942, after a visit to his native Igatpuri, Sir Henry Gidney came down with a heat stroke, and died in Delhi. He was buried in the quiet, leafy Prithviraj cemetery.

The Anglo-Indian community that he served with such love, good humour and empathy remembers him to this day as one of the greatest men to have emerged from its folds.

—Errol O'Brien

MY MOTHER INDIA

Nellie Bella O'Brien (1891–1969)

Each year, when India's Independence Day comes around, on August 15, I find myself thinking of my great grandmother—my father's paternal grandmother, Nellie Bella O'Brien.

Nellie was born into a well-to-do Bengali Christian family. She lived at various times in Jalpaiguri in north Bengal, and Dharamtolla and Jamir Lane, in Kolkata. She married Daniel O'Brien, a second-generation Irish settler (Anglo-Indian) in India, but was widowed early, while still in her twenties, and left with five children to bring up. Unusual for the times she lived in, she took up the study of medicine. Her training as a doctor—she was among the earliest women to enter medical college in Bengal—enabled her to establish a flourishing practice.

Her reputation as a woman and as a doctor was formidable. In the mid-1940s, during the Great Calcutta Killings and the pre-Partition riots, she would walk down by the railway lines that stretched from Sealdah to Ballygunge, tending to the injured. She was never harmed, neither by Hindus nor by Muslims. The stethoscope around her neck established her credentials; the determined walk established her purpose. She would not be stopped; she would not be moved till she had helped each person who came her way.

With her earnings as a doctor, she built the family home at Jamir Lane. It was a large, bustling household where three generations of the O'Brien family grew up. This house forms part of my earliest memories.

When Nellie died in 1969, I was an eight-year-old schoolboy. Yet even by then she had become an influential figure for me—the matriarch, caring but firm, who made sure my brothers and I learnt to value and understand the Indian part of our heritage.

To me, Nellie symbolized history. She was a walking, talking monument of history. To my innocent eyes, she seemed to stand for Mother India: a venerable figure who shed a silent tear first in August1947, when one country became two nations, and when a composite society was split forever.

Nellie cried every day after that till she passed away. She cried for the line that Partition drew in the hearts of two communities. She mostly cried for Patrick, her first-born, her beloved son who chose to stay on in Pakistan.

India's Partition narrative has been dominated by the subcontinent's Hindus and Muslims. Christians have had only a small role. Anglo-Indians—the community I belong to and which makes up a minuscule section of India's Christians— have had just a walk-on part.

Yet Partition had a dramatic impact on my extended family. My paternal grandfather, Amos, was Nellie's second son. Patrick, the eldest, was a civil servant who worked in Peshawar and Lahore, and served as personal assistant to Sir Olaf Caroe, Governor of the North-west Frontier Province and later with Sir George Cunningham. One day, without quite realizing its implications, these wings of the O'Brien family became citizens of separate countries when Patrick chose not to come to India on its Partition. Much of the rest of the family was settled in Kolkata.

Within months of Independence, India and Pakistan were at war. Patrick had a large family in Pakistan. One of his daughters, Doreen, married a fighter pilot who stayed on in the Indian Air Force. His brother, also a fighter pilot, opted for the Pakistani Air Force.

Imagine Doreen's plight. Night after night she stayed up, I've been told, wondering if her husband would come home, or if her brother-in-law was safe—or if these two men, brothers and comrades in the same air force till only a few months earlier, would battle each other in the eerie anonymity of the skies.

Thankfully, neither died in that war. But an insurmountable distance emerged. Mother and son, father and daughter, my Indian grandfather and his Pakistani brother—they lost touch.

Life moved on, and in the 1960s, my brothers, Andy and Barry, my cousins, Craig, Erica, Gary and I grew up knowing about this great sadness that permeated our Grandmother Nellie's soul. Ours was a truly multicultural, multi-religious upbringing. We were the only Christian family in a middle-class, predominantly Bengali-Hindu neighbourhood in Kolkata, living, in one of those ironies that make India just so captivating, in a lane named after a Muslim. We lived in the house Nellie had built in 1938.

When Nellie Bella O'Brien died at the ripe old age of seventy-eight, she was surrounded and mourned by her children, grandchildren and great-grandchildren. All of Jamir Lane, it seemed to us, had turned out for her funeral. She wasn't just my father's grandmother, she belonged to everybody. The only one missing was Patrick, the son the mother had not seen for twenty-three years.

Time passed. In 1984, my brother Andy, then a sports journalist, travelled to Karachi for the hockey Champions Trophy. We all knew the story of Patrick and his family. Andy was determined to trace the lost O'Briens. Eventually he found some living in Lahore and some others in Karachi. Patrick was dead, but the rest of the family greeted their Indian cousin very warmly. They continued to refer to the Jamir Lane residence in Kolkata as 'home'. Nellie was a legend for her grandchildren there as well, notwithstanding the fact that none had ever met her.

Nevertheless there were sobering realities. Most of the O'Brien men of my father's generation had migrated to England or Canada. The women who had remained behind and married locally, had converted to Islam.

Andy came home and told us the strange and somber story of the Muslim Anglo-Indian clan—or maybe it should be the Muslim Irish-Bengali clan—of Pakistan. We sat in silence trying to digest it. I thought of our life in India, the freedom we have to go to church and to practise our faith, the freedom that my country gives its minorities and to me as an individual to be myself. I've never felt prouder of being an Indian.

I think about my cousins in Pakistan now and then. Would they be able to join a mainstream political movement, as I have done? Would they find the opportunity to go to Parliament as regular politicians?

I was fortunate, I guess. I was fortunate because Nellie taught us to integrate with the larger community. She made sure my brothers and I learnt Bengali. She told us to be part of the *para* Saraswati Puja, saying, 'It's a celebration of wisdom and learning'. I was fortunate because India, and Bengal, allowed me to do all this without making unfair demands on me.

I was fortunate to have been nurtured by India's Nellie— and Nellie's India.

—DEREK O'BRIEN

THE QUIET INTELLECTUAL

Francis Joseph Charles Friend-Pereira
(1908–1958)

One area in which many Anglo-Indians have repeatedly excelled, is education. As teachers, they have inspired generations of students and shaped their thought processes and personalities. Friend-Pereira, a quiet, scholarly man, who was one of the foremost teachers and educationists of his time, was one such person.

He began his career as a professor of English at the University of Calcutta and went on to become the principal of Presidency College, Kolkata, one of the premier institutes for the liberal arts in India.

Friend-Pereira did his schooling at St Joseph's (North Point), Darjeeling where he was recognized as a brilliant student. He was a popular, cheerful and witty boy, and an active participant in debates and theatricals. He was a member of the First Eleven in football and hockey but his favourite sport was cricket.

After finishing school, he studied philosophy at Louvain University, Belgium, and then went to Christ Church College, Cambridge, where he took his Tripos and obtained a First Class in English, in 1939. The Tripos was divided into two parts at Cambridge. Part one was a broad-based study of the subject. Part two was a specialization within the student's chosen field. For an Anglo-Indian student to pass the Tripos in that day and age was no mean achievement.

On his return to India in 1939, Friend-Pereira joined the Bengal Government Education Service and was appointed professor of English at the University of Calcutta. To be eligible for a permanent cadre in the Provincial Service he had to pass a stiff oral and written examination in the regional language, which he did commendably.

From that point, his career as a teacher progressed spectacularly. Not only did he have a deep understanding of his subject, he had a pulse on the students' way of thinking. Perhaps he did not have the flamboyance of Derozio, but he was an inspiring figure for the boys and girls in his own way.

Friend-Pereira's disarming charm cast a spell on all who came in contact with him. His students were welcomed to his home, where they enjoyed talking and discussing everything with him, from literature to philosophy to life. His light-hearted banter and the charming anecdotes he related as they sat around the tea table were a joy to listen to. Perhaps many did not even realize at the time that among them sat the best teacher and mentor any of them would ever know, till years later when they looked back on those college days with yearning.

On 12 August 1947, he was appointed principal of the Islamia College (now known as the Maulana Azad College). His students loved him, and he was always accessible to all.

He was greatly respected by his faculty, and his endearing and warm demeanour was appreciated by all who came in contact with him.

Later, in 1955, he was appointed principal of Presidency College, a post which he held till his passing away in 1958.

As a renowned scholar and educationist, many more responsibilities came his way, and he fulfilled each role with diligence and vigour. He was president of the Hindu School Managing Committee and a member of the Calcutta University Senate. He was also a part of the West Bengal Board of Anglo-Indian Education.

Friend-Pereira loved writing poetry. Though he was never a widely published poet, the cadence and rhythm of his verse vividly expressed his love for nature and God.

One of his finest was 'Glory', written during his college days at Louvain and later published in a book of poems called *From Never in Darkness*. In the few lines quoted below the simplicity of his language brings out his piety.

> Would I had seen the wondrous glory breaking
> Over the hills of Bethlehem that night
> When choirs of angels with their songs awaking
> Shepherds, flooded the hills around with light!
> Would I had seen the Magi rare gifts taking
> O'er deserts, hills and seas, with strange insight,
> Unto the Glory that they knew was making
> Leagues to seem short and burdens to seem light.

When he passed away in 1958, his many students and colleagues were left bereft. In this obituary by an ex-pupil, John J. Pinto, we see the picture of a man who exemplified the very best of the community he came from, and who excelled as a teacher.

He was impressive without the wish to be impressive because from first to last he was a natural, so little conscious of what he was. When we recall to mind his sparkling wit, his rich sense of humour, his learning, his academic success, we will not see with our mind's eye the Professor and Principal clothed with the glamour of position; we will see the fine figure of a man with his smiling face, attentive and patient ears, quiet voice, which once stirred our feelings with cheer.

He illuminated what he touched and made lucid what he taught...Prayer and piety! These were the sources of his strength, of his contentment that ever was with him. Nothing could disturb his inner calm and tranquility that comes with grace from a clear conscience, from sincere and honest motives.

—ERROL O'BRIEN

THE STRACEY FAMILY

Anglo-Indian families, once upon a time, were large, raucous, lively units. The Straceys were one such family. There were eleven siblings—enough to make up a hockey team! Present generations of the family live outside India, and what remain in the country are the tombs bearing illustrious names and a school, the Stracey Memorial School, all in Bangalore. The story of the family is astonishing for the sheer number of people of eminence that came from it in one generation. Much of the history narrated here was told to me by Christine Kurien (nee Stracey) daughter of Ralph Stracey, who lives in the USA.

THE FORESTER

Patrick Stracey (1906-1977)

Patrick Stracey was one of India's first wildlife conservationists. A lover of nature and an accomplished forest officer, Patrick was born on 30 January 1906, in Coconada (now Kakinada) in what was then known as the Madras Presidency.

His father was a forest officer, and Patrick decided early to follow in his father's footsteps. His early education was at St Joseph's European High School, Bangalore. He was a fairly good student academically and a very promising sportsperson. Games and athletics interested him the most and he played a number of sports very well. In a strange turn of events, when he was just out of school, he was wrongly diagnosed with a heart condition which prompted him to give up sports. He went on to do an Honours course in Geology from Presidency College, Chennai.

He wrote the examination for entry into the Indian Forest Service and was ranked fifth. He topped the minority community list, yet was nearly denied entry into the service due to some political machinations. Sir Henry Gidney, the leader of the Anglo-Indian community, however, intervened on his behalf and Patrick entered the service he had set his heart on since childhood.

His first posting was in Assam. Here he worked with the great wildlife conservationist, E. P. Gee, and among other achievements, revived the rhino sanctuary at Kaziranga with Gee.

From the field, Patrick next moved to a teaching position at the Forest Research Institute, Dehra Dun, where he was put in charge of training future forest officers. Here he was known as a passionate teacher with a great love for the outdoors. He introduced a course in wildlife preservation in the 1940s, the manual of which is still in use. He returned years later to this institute as the Director of Forest Education.

In an article published online, Patrick's brother, Eric, writing about Patrick, mentions the many women who came into his brother's life. The greatest tragedy of his life came from here too. He married Ruth Beatty, a music teacher, in 1938. Eric Stracey writes in his tribute to his brother on www.aanemane.org:

> The marriage was short-lived for Ruth soon left for England to be with her parents, who had emigrated earlier, for the birth of her baby. It was a girl whom she named Pamela, but three years after she was born they made the fatal mistake of returning prematurely by sea during the height of the war, when the threat of German submarines had not yet been overcome, They touched at Rio de Janeiro where Ruth posted Pat a photo of the little girl standing on deck carrying her doll. It was to be his last glimpse of her, for the ship was torpedoed off South Africa and both mother and daughter were drowned. Pat never ceased to blame himself for allowing them to risk the voyage, and was drawn thereafter to every little girl he happened to meet, seeing in her the only daughter he had ever had, and lost.

Patrick went on to marry twice after this, but never had any children, which his brother writes was a great disappointment for him.

Even after retirement, Patrick was requested by the state government of Nagaland to serve as an advisor on forestry. He was also invited to Ethiopia to help plan their animal protection programmes. He spent four years there. It was during this period that he wrote his books *Elephant Gold; Reade, The Elephant Hunter; Nagaland Nightmare* and *The Authoritarian Tiger.*

He finally settled down in Bangalore, where he returned to help his brother Ralph, who was in failing health, to run the Stracey Memorial School.

Patrick was diagnosed with cancer of the pancreas a few years after coming to Bangalore. Not one to let something like this defeat his spirits, he refused to lie around waiting for it to spread. Instead, he packed his bags and set out for Madhya Pradesh to study the lives of forest tribal communities. The strain was, however, too much, and he passed away in Bangalore at the age of seventy-one.

In his article, Eric Stracey pays this touching tribute to his much older brother:

> As a posthumous and well-deserved honour which he would have accepted as the best and final appreciation of his services, the Board of Trustees of the World Wildlife Fund included him along with nine other conservationists in its Roll of Honour. I, who benefited much from his self-sacrifice, will always cherish the memory of his strength of character, his kindness of heart, his vivid and dynamic personality, his loyalty to the family, his ready praise, his lively conversation and his unbounded enthusiasm for life.

THE CIVIL SERVANT

Ralph Stracey (1909-1975)

Ralph Stracey was the next Stracey boy, after Patrick. He was educated, like all his brothers, at St Joseph's College in Bangalore, and was an outstanding student. He, too, graduated from Presidency College, Chennai.

In 1942, Ralph entered the Indian Civil Services. His first postings were in Chittagong, Barisal and Dhaka in the erstwhile East Bengal. A later transfer brought him to Kalimpong as a Sub-Divisional Magistrate. He was also posted in Howrah, near Kolkata, in 1946, at the peak of the communal troubles preceding India's independence.

After fifteen years in the administrative services, he resigned his commission disappointed at the growing political interference in the officers' work. He joined the Imperial Tobacco Company (ITC) as a Labour Advisor in Kolkata.

Ralph Stracey's foray into the field of education began in Kolkata in 1955. He was a member of a club called the Grail Club and felt that since the premises were not being used during the day, it could be used as a school building till 3 p.m. everyday. The school would help educate underprivileged children, particularly those from the Anglo-Indian community.

This was how the Park English School started. The school was run by a board. Subsequent boards still take care of its policies and guide the school even today.

In 1964, Ralph retired and settled in Bangalore. Enthused by his experience with education in Kolkata he decided to start a school here, and so began the Stracey Memorial School. His first student was an Anglo-Indian boy who had been denied admission at Bishop Cotton Boys' School.

The Stracey name continues to be remembered in Bangalore because of this school.

HIS MAJESTY'S ANTAGONIST

Cyril John Stracey (1915-1988)

Cyril Stracey began his career in the army when he was

posted with the first 14th Punjab Regiment to Malaya in 1941. World War II was raging, and the Japanese army was sweeping through the Far East. With their superior air power and on the ground artillery, they demolished whatever British opposition stood in their way. The British forces in Malaya, together with the Indians within the ranks surrendered, and the Indians too became Japanese prisoners of war.

Into this war-stricken zone came Netaji Subhas Chandra Bose with a vision to strengthen the Indian National Army (INA) formed to force the British out of India. Many recruits for the army came from the Indian prisoners of war held by the Japanese.

Indian officers joined the ranks of the INA but for an Anglo-Indian to be associated with the movement was a momentous decision. Eric Stracey says in his book *Growing Up in Anglo-India:*

> Cyril was not the sort of person to mindlessly follow the natural course expected of Anglo-Indians and side automatically with the British, nor would he have wanted to incur the sneers and contempts of his other Indian colleagues for a member of a community they already regarded as the lackeys of the Raj.

Cyril Stracey was given the rank of an Adjutant-General within the INA. The unit he was put in charge of, however, did not see active warfare.

There is one recorded meeting of Cyril with Netaji Subhas Bose, that occurred in August 1945. Cyril had designed a memorial to be erected for the fallen heroes of the movement. Netaji asked him to complete the building of the structure before the British landed in Singapore, as the tide of war had now turned in their favour.

The 25 feet obelisk was completed in record time. It bore the motto of the INA: *Itmad, Itefaq, Qurbani* (Faith, Unity and Sacrifice). Unfortunately, it was destroyed when the British retook Singapore.

With the defeat of the INA, Cyril was one of those put on trial for anti-British activities.

The trial of the INA prisoners of war has been well recorded. It caused a massive stir and provided a further impetus to the independence movement. Mahatma Gandhi, Pandit Nehru and Vallabhbhai Patel stepped in to defend these men while the entire world looked on.

Finally a settlement was reached with the Viceroy, and the trials were abandoned. The officers were, however, not taken back into the Indian Army. There was loss of service and emoluments.

After independence, Nehru fulfilled a promise he made to Cyril during the trials, and had him inducted into the Indian Foreign Service. Cyril went on to become Ambassador to Finland and Madagascar.

THE GUARDIAN OF THE LAW

Eric Stracey (1920-)

Eric Stracey was an upright and outstanding officer in the police services who served with rigorous honesty and bravery. He joined the police service in 1942, and his first posting was in the subdivision of Erode, Tamil Nadu.

By a strange quirk of fate he was transferred to Bengal between the years 1945 and 1946 and was put in charge of questioning INA prisoners of war recaptured by the British Army. The irony was that his brother Cyril was one of the INA men put on trial by the British.

Eric was also an inspiring teacher when he was posted at the police training school in Mt. Abu. His IPS trainees regarded him as a great motivator.

His later career was filled with turmoil as he was overlooked for promotions because he was not one to bend rules. Eric also never hesitated to reprimand senior officers.

He fulfilled his responsibilities as District Superintendent and Inspector General of Police in Tamil Nadu with courage and conviction, being noted for his ability to defuse volatile situations, particularly in his dealings with the Moplah community.

Eric Stracey ended his career as Director of Vigilance and Anti Corruption, a most unenviable task as the scourge of dishonesty had already set in, in many high places. On retirement he migrated to Australia in order to be close to his family. He wrote two books, *Growing up in Anglo-India* and *Odd Man In*. His accounts of his family particularly his brothers, provide for fascinating reading even today.

In an article on the Stracey family, S. Muthiah writes in the *Hindu*:

Apart from the four brothers, there were three sisters who survived from the eleven children born in the Stracey family. Doreen, the eldest of the girls, qualified both as a classical pianist and as a doctor. In the latter role she headed several district hospitals in the United Provinces. After serving in the Indian Army Medical Corps during World War II, she sailed for England

and practised in London till she was eighty. Margaret became a Private Secretary in the corporate sector, then a nurse before marrying a Proprietary Planter. And Winifred, who graduated from Lady Willingdon Teachers' Training College, Madras, taught in various private schools in India, including Baldwin's, Bangalore and St Hilda's, Ooty, and later in England.

—Errol O'Brien

THE CAPTAIN OF THE COMMUNITY
Frank Anthony (1908–1993)

The Anglo-Indian community has produced men and women who have excelled in diverse fields. However, two men were its most distinguished leaders—people who did remarkable work to secure the community's place within Indian society. They fought relentlessly to help it retain its dignity and to maintain its distinct character and culture. Sir Henry Gidney and Frank Anthony were these two men, and their aim was the protection and upliftment of the Anglo-Indian community.

Sir Gidney was the first leader of the Anglo-Indians to place before the governments of the day specific concerns and demands related to the community. He was the president of the All-India Anglo-Indian Association and was succeeded by Frank Anthony.

Anthony was born in Jabalpur on 25 September 1908. Educated at Nagpur University, he was a topper in English, for which he received the Viceroy's medal. He studied law in

England and was called to the Bar from the Inner Temple, one of the four Inns of Court in London. An astute lawyer, Anthony fought spirited battles in the National Defence Council, presided over by the then Viceroy Lord Wavell, concerning the difference in salaries between European and Indian commissioned officers. As a result of his advocacy, not only the salaries of Anglo-Indian officers but also those of officers of all communities were made equal to that of their British counterparts serving in India.

In India, he continued his work with the law, and was a member of the Central Legislative Assembly in 1942-'46 and a member of the Constituent Assembly. In the years before independence, Frank Anthony was deeply disturbed by the Muslim League's demand for Partition and was bitterly opposed to it. Partition, he felt, would disturb forever India's multiethnic character and inflict sufferings on the minorities for generations to come.

He put the case of his community to Mahatma Gandhi, Jawaharlal Nehru and Sardar Vallabhbhai Patel, urging these leaders to accept the Anglo-Indians as one of India's national assets. 'Although numerically small, the Anglo-Indian has given his life blood to nurture the major Indian services,' he said to them.

Anthony's intervention resulted in a special provision being inserted in the Constitution granting Anglo-Indian representation in the state and central assemblies. The Lok Sabha, the Lower House of Parliament, has, till today, two nominated seats for members of the community.

Anthony believed firmly that the Anglo-Indian community's welfare lay in acknowledging the Indian aspect of its heritage and in finding its future by staying in India. At an annual meeting of the All-India Anglo-Indian Association, he advised: 'Let us cling to all that we hold dear, our language, our way of life and our distinct culture, but let us always remember that we are Indians. The community is Indian. It has always been Indian... The more we love and are loyal to India, the more will India be loyal to us.'

Once asked if Anglo-Indians should seek special privileges as a community and be treated as a backward class, he forcefully replied: 'We are a FORWARD community... It would be a degradation, and untenable, to identify the community with the so-called untouchables in a caste-ridden society.'

Among his many writings, Anthony's book *Britain's Betrayal of India: The Story of the Anglo-Indian Community* is considered to be one of the best chronicles about his people. It is a brilliantly researched history narrated by an insider, taking the reader on a journey from how the community was born to the achievements of its many members despite the challenges and difficulties it faced over the years and in the newly independent country.

In October 1948, Frank Anthony was one of the principal delegates representing the country in the first delegation from independent India to the United Nations. In 1957, he was one of India's representatives to the Commonwealth Parliament Conference. Except for two terms, he was the nominated representative of the Anglo-Indian community in the Lok Sabha (from the first till the tenth except the sixth and ninth). Anthony's lack of political ambition was evident to all when he declined the post of Governor of Punjab and later that of the Vice-President of India when they were offered to him. He was sure that he could do better for his people by enhancing their educational status, for which he worked tirelessly throughout his life.

Anthony was elected Chairman of the Inter-State Board of Anglo-Indian Education in 1947. He fought for the rights of all minorities in the field of education—this was his greatest legacy. He was against the imposition of Hindi on non-Hindi speaking people and advocated that the language of instruction should be English.

In 1972, the Senior Cambridge Examination for schools was dropped and Anthony proposed an alternative to the government in the form of the Indian Certificate Secondary Examinations to be conducted by the Council for the Indian School Certificate Examinations. This proposal was accepted and many English-medium schools in India sought affiliation. The transfer was ratified by a Special Act of Parliament, allowing the council to run its examinations on an all-India basis; the system remains even today. Anthony was the Chairman of the Indian School Certificate board from 1958 to 1993.

The education of children and the training of teachers from the Anglo-Indian community were issues particularly close to Anthony's heart. He founded the All-India Anglo-Indian Educational Trust, which owns and manages four schools named after him in Kolkata, New Delhi and Bangalore.

Thanks to his efforts for the upliftment of Anglo-Indians, Frank Anthony was and remains one of the most luminous lights of the community. His legacy lives on today in the schools he founded, the education system he helped give shape and, through these, in the lives of every young Indian.

—ERROL O'BRIEN

BEYOND THE CALL OF DUTY

Percy Carroll (1910–1959)

In a chronicle of the lives of some of the brightest names of the Anglo-Indian community living in India, it is not only the famous and the distinguished who find a place, but the stories of little-known men and women who served beyond their call of duty deserve to be narrated too. They may not be as widely remembered today, but their lives are no less inspiring. Percy Carroll was one such man. His extraordinary courage, determination and commitment to his duty need to be recorded and remembered. This piece by his son-in-law, does just that.

—EDITOR

'True heroism is remarkably sober, very undramatic. It is not the urge to surpass all others at whatever cost, but the urge to serve others at whatever cost.'—Arthur Ashe

In 1929, a young Anglo-Indian called Percy Carroll joined the Indian Railways, or the Bengal Nagpur Railways of the time, at the age of nineteen. He was a slim, soft-spoken man with a quick smile and a rugged exterior. He joined the Railways as a driver, a job he came to love deeply. Driver Carroll was respected for his devotion to duty and loved by all. For those who worked under him, he was a tough taskmaster, yet they also saw how demanding he was on himself in discharging his responsibilities. He had to undergo some major surgeries through his adult life, but he never complained.

After joining as a trainee driver, gradually he rose to the top and was appointed as driver of the Bombay-Calcutta Mail. The fastest trains available were used on this route. Only very skilled and experienced drivers were chosen to be specially trained to operate these engines. Percy was a part of this elite group.

He proved himself more than worthy for the task at hand. On 20 March 1959, Carroll was driving the train towards Mumbai. At Chakradharpur, in what is now Jharkhand, as the engine was accelerating to reach the maximum speed after receiving the all-clear signal, Carroll spotted an obstacle on the track. A goods train had crashed into another one on the same track, causing the wagons to obstruct the tracks of the Bombay Mail. Percy had to make a split-second decision. If he hesitated for a moment he would crash into the wreckage of the two goods trains, causing death and injury to a large number of passengers. He could jump to safety but that would have resulted in even greater casualties. Being the person that he was, his only thought was on how to save his passengers.

Oblivious of his own safety and conscious only of his duty, he jammed on the breaks and hung on while shouting to his men, 'Jump for your lives! I will save the train.' He did not once consider jumping and saving his own life, instead, he stayed with 'his' engine and operated the brakes with as much power as he could apply. As a result of his action, the speed of the train was significantly reduced. However, the deceleration force was so great that it caused the engine to run off the tracks and fall down an embankment. The first car, which was carrying goods got derailed, but the rest of the train miraculously held the tracks and came to a shuddering halt.

Carroll was severely injured, and when the first rescuers tried to pull him out, they found that his crushed and bleeding leg lay beneath the twisted steel foot-plate and girders. Water gushing out from the boiler loosened the dirt and enabled them to dig him out from under the engine. A doctor travelling on the train was called to the scene to apply a tourniquet and provide immediate treatment. This kept him alive long enough to be taken to the hospital. He fought valiantly for his life, and doctors did all they could to save him, even going to the extent of amputating his leg. But ultimately he succumbed to his injuries and passed away two days later. Driver Carroll had succeeded in saving the lives of his crew and hundreds of passengers, for there were no other casualties of this horrific accident, but in so doing he sacrificed his own life. He died a hero.

As he lay battling for life, scores of people of all ages, castes and faiths, including passengers from the train called at the hospital to enquire of his condition. When he passed away, the news of his death caused the entire town of Chakradharpur to shut down in grief. Thousands of people, including schoolchildren, mourned his tragic death. Massive crowds attended his funeral.

Carroll left behind a grieving wife and six children, three of whom were then of school-going age. His wife later recalled sadly, 'About three years ago he was offered a Locomotive Inspector's job—a position that would reduce stress and risk but he refused, saying, "I love my engine and will never give up driving."'

Percy Carroll was a true hero and was awarded the Ashoka Chakra Class II for his bravery. When he died while doing his job and having saved the lives of hundreds of passengers, his words spoken some years before came to pass: 'God has asked me for a life of sacrifice. I'll give it.'

The Railways, his community, and his country need to forever remember the remarkable story of this man.

—RONALD FORBES

This article was first published in the *Indian Railways Magazine* in 2011

TWO CENTENARIANS

Leslie Charles Hart (1911–2012)
Florence St Clair Watkins (1912–)

'Fairy tales will come true
It can happen to you
If you are young at heart
And if you should survive till a 105
Look at all you derive out of being alive'

—'Young at Heart' by Frank Sinatra

Indians and centuries seem to have an affinity. Sachin Tendulkar hit hundred 100s. Fauja Singh ran the London Marathon at the age of 101. Manohar Aich of Kolkata who was called India's Pocket Hercules and was a former Mr Universe completed 100 years of age. Zohra Seghal, the actress, made this wish on her hundredth birthday: 'I wish to have long blonde hair, an hour-glass figure and a height of 5ft. 6 inches.'

Let us meet two Anglo-Indians who have hit the magical three-figure mark.

LESLIE CHARLES HART

On Valentine's Day, 1911, Leslie Charles Hart was born in what was the capital of India then, Calcutta. He had four elder siblings: three brothers and a sister. They were a fairly well-to-do family, with their father running a successful business in Amritsar.

Hart did his elementary schooling in Mussoorie and completed his secondary education from Flanders Smith College in Nainital. After this, he returned to the city of his birth, where he graduated from St Joseph's College, Bow Bazar. After a brief stint at the General Post Office, Kolkata, he decided it was time to look for a better job.

His eldest brother, Foster, was already employed in the Patna police force. With some assistance from him, Hart joined the Indian Police Service and obtained a job in Patna with the Special Branch in 1934. The Special Branch was part of the Central Intelligence Department (CID), where Hart got his basic foundation and training as a police officer.

Soon after this, the state of Bihar was divided into Bihar and Orissa and both Leslie and his brother, Foster, opted to serve in the new state of Orissa. This move proved to be very fortuitous for Leslie, for it was in Cuttack that he met, fell in love with, and married, his lovely wife Ivy Letticia (nee Cooke), who also served in Orissa as principal of Stewart School, Cuttack for thirty-five years.

Hart had a long and illustrious career as a police officer with the CID Special Branch in Cuttack. He played in the top police hockey team as right full-back, and was an excellent marksman, winning many shooting competitions during his career.

In order to secure a promotion, Leslie was told that he would have to leave the Special Branch and do a stint in the districts of Orissa. Many of his friends and colleagues tried to dissuade him from taking on this responsibility and expressed their doubts as to how he, an Anglo-Indian, would be able to carry out administrative work in the districts of Orissa. However, not being one to back down, he took up the challenge and was posted in Dhenkanal and Angul districts of Orissa as Additional Superintendent of Police. It was here that he learnt to read, write and speak Oriya fluently. He also came to be known as being extremely fair in all his dealings and was very popular with his colleagues as well as the local populace.

His next posting was as Superintendent of Police, Sambhalpur. While he was S.P. at Sambhalpur, the First Commission of the famous Hirakud Dam took place. His postings in the districts ended when he was recalled to the Special Branch in Cuttack.

His determination, tenacity and indefatigable hard work throughout his career paid off and he received all three police medals that are awarded—the Victory Medal, the Indian Police Medal for Meritorious Service and the President's Police and Fire Service Medal.

Hart retired in 1968 as the Deputy Inspector General of the Special Branch (CID), Orissa.

Besides sports, Hart's other hobby is homeopathy and he is a certified homeopathic doctor. He is a God-fearing Christian and served the Anglican Church of the Epiphany, Cuttack, as well as St Peter's Church, Kodaikanal, as a licensed lay reader, where he'd conduct and preach at Sunday services.

Hart lived with his only daughter, Gillian Rosemary Hart, former Anglo-Indian MLA (West Bengal), and Principal, Director and CEO of the Welland Gouldsmith Schools, Kolkata. In his twilight years, Leslie Charles Hart was still tall, good looking and distinguished, whose contribution to police work and to his country and community will always be remembered with respect, affection and special gratitude.

At 100 years of age, his wonderful sense of humour remained intact and he would say, 'I worked for thirty-two years in the police force, but am now drawing a pension for over forty years!' Sadly, on 18 November 2012, Hart passed away in Kolkata. This essay is my tribute to the man and his indomitable spirit.

FLORENCE ST CLAIR WATKINS

Florence St Clair Watkins was an angel of mercy for British soldiers in the Middle East during World War II and for Indian soldiers during the Chinese aggression of 1962.

Born into a family of five brothers and sisters, Watkins was educated at Jesus and Mary Convent, Bombay (Mumbai) and then at Loreto Convent, Lucknow.

The family settled in Jabalpur in 1937. Much like her namesake Florence Nightingale, as a child, instead of playing with dolls, her attention lay in toy syringes and stethoscopes.

Florence was commissioned into the Military Nursing Services on 8 August 1940. Between the years 1940 and 1945 she served in the Middle East where the horrors of war unfolded everyday in her presence.

In 1946, she received a certificate of appreciation from the Commander–in–Chief of the Middle East Forces.

In 1947, she was the Sister-in-Charge at the Combined Military Hospital at Cambellpore, now in Pakistan. The temperature had reached 112°F in that area. No air conditioning was available. Directing her staff to cool the place with buckets of water and utilizing sponges they nursed back to health fifty-two cases of heatstroke. There was no loss of life. Her services were recognized and she received the Royal Red Cross Medal Class II for her meritorious service.

During the Chinese aggression in 1962, between October and November of the year, she was the Principal Matron at the Shillong Hospital in Assam (now Meghalaya). Some 200 wounded Indians entered the hospital at all hours, day and night. Assisted by twenty-seven nurses and voluntary aides from different countries, she was always there to nurse them back to health and never left them without seeing to their assistance and comfort.

She was awarded the prestigious Florence Nightingale Medal by the International Red Cross, Geneva for outstanding devotion to the cause of nursing during the war. It was given to her by the then President Dr S. Radhakrishnan.

Watkins retired from service on 6 April 1969.

From 1972 to 1985 she was nominated by the Chief Minister of Madhya Pradesh to represent the Anglo-Indian community in the Legislative Assembly of that state. She served the community with the same grace and dedication as she did her nursing job.

She celebrated her hundredth birthday on 6 April 2012. Even in her hundredth year she has crystal clear memory, lucid expression and to listen to anecdotes from her life in the army is a joy and privilege!

—Errol O'Brien

TWO POLICE OFFICERS

Sydney Noel deSilva (1915–1990)
Ronnie Moore (1923–)

Anglo-Indian men have served in the administrative and police services in India for a long time. To include them all in this short piece would not be possible. I have chosen from among them two noble and larger-than-life officers who served their badges with pride.

SYDNEY NOEL DESILVA

Sydney Noel deSilva was an army man and police officer who served a long and distinguished career in the services, fulfilling every role he was given with diligence and dignity.

DeSilva was born in Chittagong (now in Bangladesh). He was the first graduate in his family at a time when pursuing higher studies was not the norm among Anglo-Indians. He obtained his Bachelor of Science degree from Government College, Chittagong.

The outbreak of World War II set this reserved and quiet youngster on a career path in the defence forces. He joined the British Indian Army as a Lieutenant.

In 1944, the Japanese had entered Kohima, Nagaland. Here they met their Waterloo and were driven back after a bitter encounter known as the Battle of the Tennis Court. General Slim and his 14th army took over the counteroffensive and deSilva followed with his regiment to liberate Burma.

The horror of the war was all around him. Many of his colleagues were tied to trees and bayoneted by the Japanese soldiers whilst others were made to run through minefields. His active service carried him from the Arakan Coast through Burma, into Malaysia and Thailand. Here he had to escort many Japanese prisoners of war to and from prison. Their discipline impressed him and he felt they were extremely good fighters but once defeated they accepted their position and carried out orders without question.

These war years left a deep impact on his psyche and he was to write in his diary: 'War has the power to dehumanize man, to remove his scruples about taking life. In the heat of combat where it is killing or be killed, survival depends on being utterly ruthless to the enemy.'

DeSilva held a permanent regular commission and rose to the rank of Captain while in the army. In April 1950, he resigned from the army and sat for the Indian Civil Service examination. He passed the exam and was accepted as an officer in the Indian Police Service. He served in this second phase of his career also with equal distinction.

His early postings were in Howrah and Asansol. He rose to the rank of Superintendent of Police for Jalpaiguri and Nadia. It was in Krishnagar that he established a friendship with the

American Bishop Louis Morrow. There he helped many who, while pig hunting, strayed over the border into East Pakistan (now Bangladesh) and got arrested. He would usually be the person who would go over to the East Pakistani side to explain the position to his counterparts in the other country.

DeSilva continued to rise in the service and received key postings, many of them in police and officer training institutes like Barrackpore, where he trained IPS officers, and Mt. Abu where he was commissioned to train IAS officers. He was also assigned duties as Director of the National Police Academy.

In the police force, he looked for absolute loyalty from his men. Care was taken to nurture this attribute by looking after their welfare and not hesitating to lend a hand to any job expected of them.

A noteworthy example occurred when the River Teesta burst its banks and flooded the Jalpaiguri area in north Bengal in 1968. Hundreds of people and thousands of cattle drowned. With so many corpses and carcasses rotting, there was great danger of an epidemic. The police were asked to tackle this gruesome condition as the other departments were paralysed.

At that time, deSilva was the Deputy Inspector General of the area. When he ordered his subordinates to carry out the operation, word came back that the men were reluctant to do so. He immediately set out, dug a pit, scattered lime and began dragging carcasses into it. Soon his men who were watching joined in. Word spread throughout the district that the Deputy Inspector General was himself involved in the clean-up operations. This galvanized everyone and soon the area was cleaned.

For deSilva's ability to control incidents of crime in the district, his maintenance of law and order during difficult periods and discipline within his force, and for his training of policemen, in August 1967, he was awarded the Police Medal by the President of India.

His life revolved completely around work, as a result of which his family life was neglected to a certain extent. He was transferred every two to three years, and he regarded transfers not as punishments but as appreciation of his abilities to administer difficult districts or to take up special assignments.

After retirement, deSilva settled down in his little flat off Ripon Street, Kolkata. He devoted himself to work in the St Vincent DePaul Society and was frequently seen in the lanes and by-lanes of that area assisting the underprivileged families in distress.

The final bugle call came to this just and faithful servant on 10 August 1990.

—ERROL O'BRIEN

RONNIE MOORE

During my school years at St Xavier's, Kolkata, Ronnie Moore was an icon all schoolboys hero-worshipped and wanted to emulate. He was our drill instructor. His rippling muscles, superb physique and awesome record at the boxing ring evoked our admiration. His stentorian voice was respected—but never feared—as he trained us in the field.

Moore's handling of rowdy crowds at football matches was a sight to be seen. He was often asked to be on duty when trouble was expected. His towering personality so intimidated the troublemakers that they would run helter-skelter, lungis tucked up and dhotis falling off.

Moore served as a police officer for many years, before he came into our lives. This beloved figure from our childhood days was born to Ben and Brigid Agnes in Asansol, West Bengal. The first of six siblings, he was named Ronald Allen. Ben Moore was a fireman in the East Indian Railway and a Great War veteran who had seen action in the Defence of Kut and Palestine.

Young Ron's life followed a pattern familiar to all Railway families in India: unusual hours; irregular transfers between Railway divisions; frequent change of schools. In the manner of Railway children, Moore knew all the East Indian Railway locomotives by class and his father's engines by number. Train times and numbers were part of everyday idiom. He had a happy childhood, racing homing pigeons, rearing fighting cocks, playing marbles, flying kites, top-spinning and using the catapult.

At eighteen, he followed his father into railway service and joined the East Indian Railway as an A-grade fireman. His mother, however, was determined that he should go into a better profession and urged him to seek another career.

So in due course he found himself at the gates of Lalbazar, the headquarters of the Kolkata police force. On 2 June 1941, Moore reported to the police training school, and began a way of life that was to last for the next thirty-six years.

Six months after joining the force, in 1942, Moore was posted to the Mounted Branch. While on late-night mounted patrol, he was struck by a tram as his horse shied into the path of a tram in the wartime blackout. His horse was killed and he was hospitalized for six weeks and incapacitated for another three months.

In 1946, he was promoted to Sergeant-Major, 'B' (Gurkha

and Hilltribes) Company, Calcutta Armed Police. The year was one of unprecedented civil violence. It began with the February riots and later on the horrendous Great Calcutta Killings unfolded in which up to 10,000 persons were believed to have died. Like all British and Anglo-Indian police officers of that period, he was actively involved in the near continuous police operations to retain order and control.

With the approach of Independence, Moore decided to stay on in independent India and serve in the police force here rather than follow in the footsteps of many fellow Anglo-Indians overseas.

In 1949, he undertook a physical training course at Pune and returned as Chief Drill Instructor at the Police Training School, being promoted to the gazetted rank of Inspector of Police. He was also the resident physical training inspector for the students of St Xavier's School.

Ronnie Moore was the recipient of innumerable awards, including the President's Police Medal for Meritorious Service in recognition of his actions in quelling the notorious Bagmari Riot in Chitpur, North Calcutta, in 1966.

The story of his professional life is a string of daring exploits. Early in his career he saved a fellow cadet from drowning in the training school tank. Then, while on duty at a trade exhibition on the Kolkata Maidan, a telephone linesman was trapped and electrocuted in the overhead powerlines. Regardless of his own safety, Moore freed the unconscious man from the live wire and resuscitated him. There is also the story of how he was called in to handle Phulmala, a rogue adult female elephant who had killed her mahout and was running amok in Kolkata's Zoological Gardens. With great sadness yet precise marksmanship he dispatched the enraged animal swiftly and efficiently.

For three decades, Ronnie Moore was possibly one of the most widely known Anglo-Indian in Kolkata. He was especially sensitive about the plight of the community and went out of his way to help and support them on countless occasions. Many found employment through his intercession and he often mediated with local police on their behalf, when in trouble. He was highly regarded in police circles as the model for a senior police officer: a disciplinarian without being a martinet; an authority on drill and ceremony without pedantry; a competent man-manager and a fearless leader in times of riots and disturbance with a patent disregard for personal safety.

His superior officers consistently showed complete faith in his actions and never failed to support his decisions.

Moore's married life was a happy one. While still a Sergeant in the Mounted Police, he married Colleen Mary Dunn, the daughter of a former senior station master on the East Bengal Railway. They had three children.

However, while being a policeman was his career, his real passion was boxing. At an early period of his career he began training at the US Army Camp, Howrah, with military policeman Master-Sergeant Lester Carter, who had been a sparring partner for the then heavyweight champion of the world, Joe Louis. He learnt much from Lester. He was such a good boxer that he was selected for the London Olympics in 1948 and the Helsinki Olympics in1952. It is only a matter of speculation now as to how he would have fared on those stages, because on both occasions the police force could not spare him and he never made it to either Olympics. He competed at the national level, though, and became the All-India Heavyweight

Boxing Champion in 1957, defeating the then title-holder Glen (Dusty) Miller.

The Kolkata police force did not forget this champion in their midst years after his retirement. When they decided to institute a boxing championship in 2005, they named the trophy after Ronnie Moore. The Commissioner of Police of the time frantically tried to persuade Moore to come down to Kolkata to present the trophy but he was settled close to his family in Australia and his age would not permit the long and arduous plane journey.

Moore still remembers his life in India vividly and with great affection, and like former policemen the world over, he reflects that one may leave the police service, but you remain a policeman in spirit to the end.

—PETER MOORE

This piece is adapted from Peter Moore's eulogy to his father, 'An Ordinary Bloke'.

THE ALOHA BOY

Garney Nyss (1916–1998)

Kolkata, in the early 1940s, was a city at war. Once the Japanese bombed Pearl Harbour and entered the Second World War, the hostilities came within India's borders.

There was a minor offloading of three bombs at various parts of Kolkata. Barrage balloons floated over the Maidan and Ack Ack guns shattered the peace of the city along Red Road, which had become an airstrip for fighter Spitfires.

American troops were all over the city to help a beleaguered British Indian Army. Yet, local entertainment did not stop. The Grail Club on Park Street had many recreational facilities spread over a sprawling complex. The Rangers Club was another happening place as was the Monsoon Square Gardens on Short Street behind St Xavier's College.

78 RPM music records stopped coming from Britain, though labels continued to be produced by the Gramophone Co. in Dum Dum.

It was into this entertainment scene that Garney Nyss and

the Aloha Boys stepped in to take the Kolkata crowds by storm. Nyss was a genius on the sliding steel guitar, coaxing out lilting tunes. His hands could also play out rapid Hawaiian beats on the guitar accompanied by rhythm guitars and ukuleles.

Kolkata's dance floors were mesmerized as the Aloha Boys adroitly turned out Hawaiian music and current hits. The group brought out over fifty records.

Nyss's passion for music continued well into his life and his appeal did not fade over the years. He continued to give performances and the Kolkata press nicknamed him the Peter Pan of music in their musical reviews.

This piece by Soutik Biswas describes the multifaceted talents of this man.

—EDITOR

I met Garney Nyss in Kolkata when he was well into his seventies. That week, the dapper septuagenarian had shot a high school reunion on his favourite Rolleiflex camera, played a game of tennis at the local club, and taught steel guitar riffs to admiring students at a music school. In between, he had walked into his publisher's office in a south Kolkata neighbourhood to discuss the layout of his forthcoming book, a picture celebration of how India looked years ago.

Photography was only one of Nyss's passions. This Anglo-Indian was one of India's niftiest hockey players. He played for Bengal for a record eighteen years and was acknowledged as the country's finest left-wing. At twenty years of age he was nearly chosen for the 1932 London Olympic hockey team, but then dropped as he was considered to be too young! He was a speed skating champion; a prime athlete clocking an admirable 10 seconds for a 100-yard run; a club league-level batsman and legspinner who played with C. K. Nayadu, and a badminton and tennis player of considerable repute. He had also taken great photographs, made fascinating documentaries, cut albums with folk and country music bands, and was an ornithologist.

What was his true métier then, I asked some who knew him well. 'He was an all-rounder par excellence, a patron saint of versatility,' Barry O'Brien said of him. He should know. In 1995, in a happy accident, he stumbled on to 'Uncle' Garney's collection of greying, dusty picture albums in his unkempt two-room Park Street apartment during a routine visit. This treasure trove of old pictures, handsome black-and-white images of Indian life and times in the 1940s, eventually found their way into *India: 50 Years Ago*, a Heritage publication sponsored by the Steel Authority of India Limited, and later published again as *Memories: A Photographic Essay of India in the 1940s*.

'I always did things which gave me pleasure. I was never a hard-boiled professional. Such things (books) are all rewards in a way,' Nyss told me. Not that he cared for rewards, anyway. He was a quintessential amateur of yore. His work—dribbling, clicking, working a riff—was that of a disciplined amateur with an exceptional eye for perfection and detail.

His father was an excise officer in the hills of Darjeeling, and Garney's love of nature began there. He was a knowledgeable bird man, and had an extensive collection of butterflies.

Growing up in the misty chill of Darjeeling also fed one other passion in Nyss—he was fascinated by the toy train chugging up the mountain everyday. On his eighth birthday, his father gifted him a Kodak Brownie box camera worth 8 rupees, and Nyss decided to capture images of the train for posterity. 'I got hooked to photography clicking trains, mountains and what not,' he recounted. Nyss's early photographs of Darjeeling were poetic black-and-white essays of clouds, mists, trains and mountain loops.

Over the years, between various jobs—as proofreader in a government press, or as a manager with the fabled Bourne and Shepherd studios in downtown Kolkata—Nyss indulged his passion with his Agfa and Ensign bellow cameras worth 30 rupees. Later on, he bought a pocket Kodak, and finally the Rolleiflex with 2.8 lenses for a steep Rs 500. In the 1930s and the '40s, Nyss made his professional mark as the photographer for weddings in Kolkata. If you were getting married and wanted a memorable album, you simply hired Nyss on the condition that you would buy minimum twelve photographs at Rs 25 apiece. Which meant Nyss was richer by at least Rs 250 for every marriage he caught on camera. 'I must have recorded thousands of weddings,' he said. 'Anglo-Indian weddings, Punjabi weddings, Bengali weddings, Marwari weddings, the works.'

Nyss was also a peripatetic bachelor, travelling all over the country by train, shooting pictures of cities and people in faithful black and white, and preserving them in albums with pithy captions. Many of these photographs appeared in the book, which is a record of the work of a mature amateur with a yen for a bare bones, stripped-down, honest photography of life with an unerring attention to detail. Nyss himself was casual about it all: 'Oh, I just went along and clicked. I loved travelling, and I loved taking pictures.'

His versatility was mind-boggling, as was his approach to the arts. His 16-mm documentaries in colour shot on a Rs 2,000 Paillard Bolex camera maybe out of circulation today, but reveal an amazing grasp over a range of subjects: a twenty-minute film on Mother Teresa, 'three reels' of the Queen's visit to India in 1960 and *Moths and Butterflies*, a twenty-minute documentary commissioned by the Government of India.

Nyss was also an accomplished musician. He burst on to the Kolkata music scene during the Second World War. Along with his group, Aloha Boys, he brought the house down singing Jim Reeves, Bing Crosby and King Cole covers as well as turning out Hawaiian tunes. His skill with the steel guitar was also an obsession that produced 500 AIR broadcasts and over a hundred albums. The Aloha Boys mesmerized the Kolkata dance floors, and when some of the boys quit the act, Nyss promptly formed The Harmonisers 'with a couple of girls'—a four-piece-guitar-drums-ukelele combo belting folk and country, Eric Clapton ballads, Neil Diamond standards to packed audiences. Nyss continued to front the band for many years working up some pretty good jams.

His use of the electric steel guitar made it popular with the Bengalis and it got used in Rabindrasangeet renditions as well as in film music. In his later years he taught the guitar at the Calcutta School of Music and was a regular performer at their musical presentations.

What did he love most? Was it playing a hot cover of the 'Tiger Rag'; capturing another vignette of the big city bustle on film; or executing a stinging backhand on the South Club tennis courts? Probably all.

—SOUTIK BISWAS

This essay is adapted from a piece written for *Outlook* magazine, published 18 August 1997.

THE RED BERETTA
Father Lawrence Trevor Picachy (1916-1992)

Father Lawrence Picachy came into my life at the beginning of the school year of 1948, as Prefect of Discipline, St Xavier's Collegiate School, Kolkata. We boys soon became familiar with his tall, well-groomed figure, as he would visit each classroom and made it a point to know everything about each student. As a result of this, he could identify every boy in the school. Right through his life, this was one of his marvellous traits: his memory of people and attention to every member of society.

Lawrence Trevor Picachy was born on 7 August 1916, in Lebong, Darjeeling. Members of the Picachy family were wardens of the Cathedral and of the Church of Our Lady of Dolours, at Baitakhana, Calcutta. His father was a doctor in Burma, and Lawrence and his brother, Eric, completed their education at North Point, Darjeeling.

Picachy joined the novitiate on 11 March 1934, and was ordained a Jesuit priest in 1947. St Xavier's College played an important part in the priestly life of Father Picachy. From 1949 to 1954, he was the Prefect of Discipline of the school. I was in school at that time and remember well how he kept our welfare in mind always. He carefully monitored the scholarly side of our school life and was a regular on the sports field too, where he would spot talent and encourage us. He was appointed Rector of St Xavier's College in 1954, a post which he held till 1958.

Courtesy was second nature to him and he had infinite patience. People from all walks of life and every community came to know and love this soft-spoken and kind priest.

In times of illnesses, he would visit the sick at home or the hospital, bringing reassurance and prayers. His hospital ministry was well known in Kolkata. Every Thursday, he would cycle down to the PG Hospital to visit the patients and the nursing staff, his presence a source of joy and peace for everyone.

I got a personal glimpse of this part of his work, and even today it evokes in me a feeling of nostalgic gratitude. My father was dying of cancer. Though by then Father Picachy was Rector of St Xavier's, he would cycle the not inconsiderable distance every week from Park Street to Ballygunge to console and reassure the family. Such was the greatness of this man.

After a successful stint as Rector of St Xavier's, he was posted at Basanti, a village in the 24 Parganas that could be reached only by launch from Canning. He flung himself into his work in the remote villages of the area with characteristic love and devotion. He travelled widely here and his visits were a treat to the children of the boarding schools in these areas. He would take with him a trunk-load of cakes and sweets, but more than that he would spend the whole day chatting with the children and sharing their simple fun and talk. The proficiency he gained in Bengali here would help him in his priestly duties later too.

In 1962, the new diocese of Jamshedpur was formed. The well-known ex-Rector of St Xavier's College seemed to be the natural choice for the Steel City. Father Picachy was named the first Bishop of Jamshedpur. The timing was opportune. The Vatican Council was on. Bishop Picachy now had to go to Rome for long periods to deliberate over various themes of the Council. His affable nature and friendly approach soon made him a popular figure among the Council of Bishops. He received invitations from prelates from various parts of the world to visit their dioceses, as he was regarded an accomplished speaker and a good communicator.

In August 1969, Bishop Picachy was nominated the Archbishop of Calcutta. For those who were to work with him, it was welcome news. He was a good leader who delegated responsibility to those deserving of it, and then helped them with their work as needed, backing them fully always. He was gentle with people in difficulty and would try to see the brighter side of any problem. At this time, he was also the spiritual advisor to Mother Teresa.

In 1976, the Bishops of India elected him President of the Catholic Bishops' Conference of India and in the same year he was honoured by Rome with the post of Cardinal.

After the solemn ceremony at the Vatican where he was elevated to cardinality, he remarked, 'My new dignity comes as a proof not only of the increasing internationalization of the Catholic Church's governing structure, but also of the emerging role of India and the Indian Catholic community.'

The Pope in turn granted him a special audience in which

he said, 'It is with honour and esteem that we extend our welcome to you. The Church in Calcutta, the People of all India are in our thoughts today. We welcome you as another representative of the culture, civilization and wisdom of India. Above all, you have come as the worthy Pastor of the Church of Calcutta, bringing with you the joy, and hope, the grief and anguish of your people.'

When the Cardinal returned to Kolkata, he was accorded a grand public welcome at the Indoor Stadium at which the Governor of West Bengal was present. The packed benches around the stadium were ample evidence of his immense popularity and the affection and esteem which the people of Kolkata had for him.

Cardinal Picachy was India's third Cardinal. He had the opportunity of being present at the sessions of the Second Vatican Council and of attending the conclaves for the election of Pope Paul I and Pope John Paul II.

He was one of the three Presidents for the Synod of Bishops on Family nominated by Pope John Paul II. He was, in fact, the first Asian to be given that honour.

Ill-health began to trouble him around the year 1983. He started having difficulty in walking. The papal visit in 1986 was the last major event in his life before retirement. He summoned all his strength to keep pace with the occasion.

He accompanied the Holy Father from the airport to Nirmal Hriday Ashram in Kalighat, Mother Teresa's Home for the Dying, and played host to the Pope in Kolkata for two days. His resignation from the position of Archbishop had already been given to the Pope and he used this occasion to impress on the Holy Father his inability to continue as Archbishop.

In May 1986, his resignation was accepted. For a short

while he went to Bangalore and was cared for by the Little Sisters of the Poor, but there he was lonely. He returned to Kolkata, to his beloved St Xavier's, and spent his last days in the same room which he had when he was the Prefect. The presence of other Jesuits and the many visitors and friends who came by gave him the companionship and affection which he enjoyed.

On 29 November 1992, Cardinal Picachy passed away at Woodlands Nursing Home, Kolkata following a cerebral hemorrhage. The funeral rites were held in the open grounds of St Xavier's College and he was buried in a newly built cemetery in Dhyan Ashram, a Jesuit training centre and retreat house 18 km outside the city.

—ERROL O'BRIEN

INDIA'S FIRST WORLD CHAMPION

Wilson Lionel Garton Jones (1922-2003)

Wilson Jones was born in Pune on 22 May 1922. In the course of a long and illustrious sports career, he won the national billiards championship twelve times, the world billiards championship twice and the national amateur snooker championship five times. He was the first Indian sportsperson to be a world champion in any sport and gave the newly independent country a tremendous sense of pride and self-belief. His exploits inspired generations of billiards players and till date Indian players of this sport are considered among the most skilled in the world.

Young Jones's initiation into billiards makes for an entertaining story. One day, when he was still a boy, he was told to go fetch his Uncle Ossie for dinner from Nobel Saloon, the club opposite the house, in Pune. The club had strict rules about allowing minors to enter. So Jones peeked in through the windows—and what he saw entranced the boy. There were coloured balls placed on a green baize table—fifteen balls placed in a triangle. He heard someone mention the word 'cannon'—but surely they did not mean a real weapon? Fascinated and further intrigued, Jones watched the cueist stretch elegantly across the table and pot a red ball. 'Hazard!' the cry went up.

So started a lifelong fascination. Jones watched the game almost everyday through the window till, at the age of seventeen, he could finally enter the club as an adult and be allowed to play a game of billiards. From then on, his schoolwork took backstage and the terminologies and rules of this game overtook all else in his life. Cannon, he learnt, meant striking a cue ball so that it hits the other cue ball and the red one on the same stroke. Hazard meant potting a ball.

Jones took to the game as though born to it and set such records at the club that his name was inscribed in its record books. He was a natural. His confident stance at the table and the easy flowing motion of the cue in his hands all came to him without the necessity of a coach. Jones's talents were impressive; he soon outgrew the challenges the club could put up for him and his fellow players suggested he move to Mumbai to gain experience and national recognition.

At this point, World War II intervened and Jones started working at the ammunitions factory at Kirkee. His tremendous capacity for hard work was greatly appreciated by officers at the factory and he was promoted to the position of a senior supervisor. Despite holding a full-time job, Jones continued to work on his billiards after work hours, training himself and honing his proficiency.

Jones's first success came at the Evening News of India Snooker Championships held at the YMCA in Byculla. His opponents were renowned players of the game and on paper his chances were slim. A bundle of nerves throughout, Jones managed to advance into the final round and beat the favourite Taher Ali. Winning the title gave Jones recognition and membership to an exclusive club. There he had the opportunity to play his game against opponents endowed with varying styles and techniques.

When World War II finally came to an end, like many others, Jones found himself unemployed. The entire country was teetering on the edge of major upheavals, with Independence and Partition just around the corner. The Anglo-Indian community was feeling particularly insecure as its members were looked upon with suspicion by many Indians.

Jones, back in Pune, spent all his time at the Deccan Gym and the Noble Saloon. He kept up with his game with a burning passion, determined to iron out his flaws and develop higher and higher degrees of skills. He visited Mumbai again in 1947 for the Evening News of India Snooker Championship. There he met Reginald Hollinson, the Superintendent of Police of the Mazagon docks. Their friendship resulted in Jones's appointment as an assistant security officer. He was promoted to the post of docks chief within a short time—he could now play on tables reserved for higher officers.

Jones soon caught the eye of Rattansey Vissanji, the owner of the Wallace Flour Mills. This was the turning point that finally set him on the path to becoming a world champion. Jones was given employment at the mills as well as boarding and lodging with his employer. He could practice on the tables at Vissanji's residence at any hour of the day.

In 1951, Jones won the Billiards National Championship. By winning the national title, he earned the Indian nomination for the World Amateur Billiards Championship. The championship was held in England where, unfortunately, Jones could not acclimatize in time. The conditions got the better of him and adversely affected his play. Yet, he made a deep impression on the media and the spectators. 'No better or more graceful loser has participated in this event. He took a drubbing but learnt from it' was how the press described him.

The London experience prompted Jones to improve his game tremendously. He won both billiards and snooker titles at the national championship in Kolkata in 1952. However, the national championship was not enough for Jones any longer— his eyes were now firmly fixed on the world title.

Jones competed on the world stage three times in four years, but it brought him no nearer to the title he so coveted. But he persevered with his training, refusing to give up. The toil and perseverance that brought him the world title is a lesson for generations of sportspeople.

Jones's son, Geoff Jones, describes his father's commitment to the game thus:

> Dad was very dedicated and devoted, with a lot of determination and self-motivation. He would spend hours everyday, practising, and before the start of the world championships, for six months he would practise for eight hours a day, everyday of the week. To crown it all, he never missed a practice session for twenty-six years.

Jones was a trailblazer for Michael Ferreira, thrice World Billiards Champion, and Pankaj Advani, the only Indian to win both Billiards and Snooker World Championships.

On 11 December 1958, Wilson Lionel Garton Jones finally won the World Amateur Billiards title. The Great Eastern Hotel in Kolkata was the venue for this historic event. In a hall packed to the brim with spectators, Jones played his last match of the series, prior to the finals, against Chandra Hirjee, a national champion. He had already defeated Tom Cleary of Australia and Leslie Driffield, the 1952 title-holder, in the preliminaries.

In billiards jargon, Jones was a fast break builder and something of a whiz kid, in that he could start from seemingly impossible situations to attain a winning position. A defeat now against Hirjee would smash his title chances. But when time was called, Jones had notched up 4,655 points against Hirjee's 2,888.

And then it was time for the final match, where he was again playing against Driffield. Somewhere midway through the match, he was languishing 662 points behind Driffield, with only 105 minutes to spare. Downcast spectators began to slip out of the hall.

Then Jones unleashed his magic touch and won an avalanche of points. With nine minutes to spare, Jones took the lead for the first time in the game. The game ended with the score: Jones 2,865; Driffield 2,729. And the hall rose as one to applaud the national hero.

'Incredible! I don't know how I did it!' was the only comment Jones could make about it even years after the event. According to him, it was the most memorable win of his career.

A person with great inner strength, Jones had an uncanny ability to get past prolonged periods of crisis—and that performance against Driffield put his name amongst the great sportsmen of the country.

Jones regarded his game at the city of Pukekohe in New Zealand as his most satisfying win abroad. This was the year 1964, and Jones made Indian sports history by becoming a world champion for the second time. The opponents were strong at every level, but the toughest game he played was against compatriot Mike Ferreira. It was a pulsating match and, though Ferreira eventually lost, he fought fiercely, making it a heart-stopping match for the spectators.

Jones's charm and striking good looks made him a memorable figure among the locals. Geoff recounts this amusing incident as proof of the impression Jones had on the people of the Kiwi town:

> In 2003, I along with my wife, Julia, and daughter, Lily, visited New Zealand and made it a point to drive to the quaint town of Pukekohe where Dad won his second crown.
>
> It was indeed a pilgrimage and, to my delight, we even met the chief referee who supervised that tournament. He was ninety-eight and was living in a home for the aged, but the moment I told him I was Geoff Jones from India it clicked and he said, 'Oh, you are the son of Wilson Jones. You're a chip of the old block.'

Jones was felicitated with a number of awards. He was given the Arjuna Award in 1962, the Padma Shri in 1965 and the Dronacharya Award in 1996. For him, though, his meeting with Prime Minister Jawaharlal Nehru was one of the most momentous events of his life.

> As I entered the room, he was behind a kidney table at work. He came up to me lightly on his feet, his eyes lit up with happiness as though he was meeting a long-lost friend and he shook my hand warmly. It was my proudest moment.

Jones married Hildreth Margaret Wade, whom he first met at the YMCA Byculla when he was playing a match there. He was a handsome, debonair man with striking silver-grey hair at the age of twenty! Smitten by the young Elizabeth, he would sit on the compound wall at Agripada, Mumbai, where Elizabeth lived, and would whistle to her. This would annoy Elizabeth's mother no end and she would complain, 'Who is that old man whistling at you?' But the competitive streak in Jones never let him give up and, eventually, the two got married. They remained by each other's side for fifty-three years.

Geoff says of his parents:

> She was indeed his queen. It is said that the greatest way a father can show his love for his children is by loving their mother. Dad loved his little family and will always remain our champion!

Geoff was Jones and Elizabeth's only child and it would forever remain a regret for Jones that he could never spend enough time at home, watching his son grow up. He would spend hours practising and many months away travelling to tournaments. But the time that he did spend with Geoff transformed into some of the most fascinating moments of the little boy's life.

> During the World Snooker Championship in Kolkata, he made me his ball boy in practice sessions, which would last for about three to four hours. It was a backbreaking job, but I thoroughly enjoyed it. To me, as a young boy, he seemed to have magic in his fingers—the way he made the balls on the table behave and listen to him! It was indeed an art that he perfected and which won him so many titles. I always felt great

pride and joy [in being] his son. More than being a world champion, he was a gentle giant, huge in frame and yet so humble and down to earth—and, above all, a fantastic human being. Never once did I hear him raise his voice. He was always the perfect gentleman and will always be my hero, Geoff says.

Jones finally called it a day in 1967. He retired as an undefeated world and national title-holder and spent the remaining years of his life as a coach. He nurtured the talents of Ashok Shandilya and Subhash Agrawal, who went on to win world billiards titles. He also mentored the great Geet Sethi, helping him correct his stance, which was hindering his play.

Wilson Jones, sportsman, gentleman, father, coach and a luminous name in the Anglo-Indian community, will always be remembered as the champion who inspired an entire country.

—ERROL O'BRIEN

A LEGEND OF THE GAME

Leslie Claudius (1925–)

'Hockey is not worthwhile watching if he is not playing. He is the greatest player in the world.'

—*The Times*, London, 1948

The Indian Railways and Railway colonies were bastions of Anglo-Indian employment. They were also the breeding ground of many sportspersons, especially hockey players who amazed the world with their incredible skills. Swashbuckling players who rose from the community represented India in the Olympics and brought home gold medals. The 1928 Indian hockey team had eight Anglo-Indian players. The 1932 and 1936 teams each had four, and right up to 1960 the community was always represented. Richard Allen, the Indian goalkeeper, had the distinction of not letting in a single goal at the 1936 Olympics.

One such player was Leslie Walter Claudius who was born

on 25 March 1925, in the Railway town of Bilaspur. Today, even the paanwalla at McLeod Street, Kolkata, will willingly direct you to his house. Once an international hockey player, this octogenarian still responds to the name his contemporaries gave him: Younker. His frail physique belies his inner strength. Quiet and unassuming, he has climbed heights of glory. His is a simple life, rich with accomplishments.

Leslie Claudius played in four consecutive Olympics from 1948 to 1960, winning three gold medals and one silver. His name is recorded in the *Guinness Book of World Records* for having won the maximum number of Olympic medals in hockey. The Indian government awarded him the Padma Shri in 1971. Thousands of miles away in London, he is treated as first among the very best players the world has ever produced. The London Olympics 2012 organizers renamed tube stations in their bustling metropolis after three of our hockey greats— Dhyan Chand, Roop Singh and Leslie Claudius. The Bushey overground station on the Orange Line was named after Leslie Claudius.

Claudius was a vibrant figure in the golden era of Indian hockey when our country prevailed supreme in the game. From his late teens, Claudius had a dream of becoming a sportsperson. He recalls: 'I was initially a footballer playing for the Bengal Nagpur Railway (BNR) team.' His career in hockey began with the 1946 Beighton Cup hockey tournament, and is a strange story of sporting serendipity.

Claudius had played for the BNR football team and even represented it at the IFA Shield. He was watching a practice session between the BNR A and B hockey teams as they prepared for the Beighton Cup, a premier hockey tournament, when the centre-half of one team fell sick. Claudius, who was on the sidelines, got a pleasant surprise when Dickie Carr, the team captain, invited him to join the team and fill the missing position. Carr had played football with Claudius, and knew his abilities as a sportsperson.

Claudius took up the challenge and entered the field. He played for the team for the next ten days. With regular coaching his flair for the game shone through and he bid farewell to football and began his hockey career.

Incidentally, the BNR team lost in the finals of the 1946 championship despite playing wonderful hockey.

Claudius played hockey when the rules had still not been changed. The start of the game was a 'bully off'. Reverse turning was penalized, and the goalkeeper wore no protective headgear and padded material around his chest.

With fondness, Claudius remembers that during the initial years he was encouraged by Olympians like Joe Galibardi, Carl Tapsell and Dickie Carr. He spent hours improving his technique, hitting throw-ins and perfecting the body swerve under their supervision.

'They even had my hockey stick cut short by three inches so that I could use it more effectively. There was no finish line. You had to build pressure on yourself. You had to work on your weaknesses,' says the hockey legend.

Some men are born with talent. Such a man was Leslie Walter Claudius. He had an exceptional flair for hockey. But talent alone will not take an individual to the top of his chosen sport. To live up to that high degree of natural talent, he had to work hard. Claudius was a glutton for work. He worked himself to the bone, perfecting a technique which led *The Times* to declare him as the 'finest player in the world'.

Even though he never played with the heroes of Indian

hockey like Dhyan Chand and Roop Singh, he has many affectionate memories of them. Commenting on Dhyan Chand or the 'Wizard of Dribble', he reminisces: 'His work was brilliant. Once I remember the spectators even examined his stick to find if there was glue on his stick.

'When I was playing, he was a selector. He called me a sparrow. He thought I was like a small bird hopping around wherever the ball was. I remember he would say, "Claudius selects himself, now I have to select the rest of the team."'

When Claudius was in his prime, the other Indian right-halves decided there was no point trying to play for this position since he owned it. And so they opted for the left-half position. Once he entered the national team, he was never benched by the selectors, and he played over 100 international matches.

He was chosen to play for the Port Commissioners as centre-half in the Aga Khan tournament in 1948 where his wonderful performance caught the eye of the selectors. Even though he had a fractured hand, he was selected for the Olympics.

Those were memorable days for the twenty-one-year-old player. According to Claudius, inspite of the absence of coaches, the Indian team was outstandingly talented. The entire team sat around a miniature replica of a hockey ground to plan out their moves. Coaches were appointed for the Indian team only in 1952.

How did Claudius get to the top and stay there for so long? The answer is simple. He studied the game closely and did a lot of homework. About the importance of practice, Claudius stresses that if a player is not prepared to work alone, and work everyday, he cannot become really good. The secret is also to be observant on and off the field. It is only by watching players closely that you can understand and imbibe the best of what they are doing. Slowly, the perfection seeps into your own game too.

His saddest playing experience was at the 1960 Rome Olympics where, in the final match between India and Pakistan, a misunderstanding between the two Indian defenders caused a lapse, and the Pakistani players took advantage of this and won by one goal. 'We played brilliant hockey. They were not the superior team. That's why its hurts,' he still rues. Soon after the Rome Olympics, Claudius retired from the game, though he continued to be associated with it in many forms for decades.

The state of Indian hockey today saddens this master greatly. It is ironic that in London, in 1948, where he once won gold for India, in 2012, India was at the bottom of the table. His was a different era. 'Oh, those were the days... We played from the heart. With K. D. Singh (Babu) we had the best team in 1952 at Helsinki. We were invincible,' he recalled in an interview.

This great player is one among the best of the many Anglo-Indians who have played for India over the years. He will always be remembered for his exceptional skills, hard work and dedication to the sport by every sports lover.

—Errol O'Brien

TWO GRAND LADIES OF KOLKATA

Sheila Broughton (1929–)
Philomena Eaton (1937–)

SHEILA BROUGHTON

On the wall, just above her desk and a little above eye level, hangs a plaque inscribed with these words: 'I shall pass through this world but once. Any good thing that I can do, or any kindness I can show any human being let me do it now, and not defer it, for I will not pass this way again.'

These words sum up neatly the vision and philosophy of Sheila Broughton, educationist and founder, Julien Day School, Kolkata.

Sheila Broughton has worked in the field of education for over fifty years, during which time she has been an inspiration to thousands of her students.

Broughton's own schooling was at St John's Diocesan School, and she completed her matriculation in 1946. Her principal was Sister Dorothy Francis during whose tenure the reputation of the school was at its zenith. Perhaps it was due to Sister Francis's influence, or that of her mother, Grace Julien, who was also a teacher, that Broughton decided to take up a career in the teaching profession. She studied for the teacher's training course at the Presentation Convent, Church Park, in Chennai in 1947-'48.

On her return to Kolkata, she started assisting her mother at her primary school at 34, Elgin Road. This school offered classes only till the junior section and was very popular. However, parents soon started asking for a senior section to be added as admission of pupils to higher classes in other schools became difficult once they completed the junior section here.

But space was a problem. Yet, Broughton was not one to give up. She convinced her landlord to lease a further portion of his property to her to be used as a school.

The foundation stone of the present Julien School was laid in 1969.

It is to be remembered that Broughton was not backed by a corporate or financial conglomerate. An individual seeking to establish a school faces many constraints, particularly with the costs.

Many parents came to Broughton's assistance and went on a fund-raising drive. Finally, they convinced the Union Bank of India to back the school financially.

Eventually, three branches of the school came up in and around Kolkata. The students from the Elgin Road branch would go often to Scout Camp at Ganganagar, beyond Dum Dum, to picnic. Broughton decided to start a school here, much to the amazement of many. When she was asked why she chose a backward village for her school, her answer was that she didn't choose Ganganagar, the place chose her. What she did not realize when she decided on the locality, was that the area was a hotbed of Naxal activity.

In 1975, the land along with the building was purchased and the school at the primary level was started in 1976. Opening the school was not easy with the local people opposing the setting up of the school unless given jobs there. However, with the help of the local MLA, the situation was brought under control. Eventually, the people of the area realized that the school was meant for their children and became wholehearted patrons of the school.

Around the years 1987-'88 a proposal to open a school in Kalyani, a town 60 km from Kolkata, came from a prominent member of the Kalyani Civic Association. He was aware of the reputation of the Julien Day School in Kolkata and was eager for a branch to be set up there. The school trust members were happy to consider this despite certain logistical problems and fears of local interference. A plot of land allocated for a high school was obtained from the government and Julien Day in Kalyani started in 1989. In the year 2007, again battling against odds, Broughton started a school in Howrah.

The various branches of the Julien Day schools now cater to about 6,000 students. A trust, set up by Broughton and others, works to ensure the education of Anglo-Indian and Christian children. Free education is given to around eighty Anglo-Indian children. Other underprivileged children also get free education.

Broughton, recounting her work with these children at Ganganagar says:

It was in the year 1973 that a school friend of mine, in the process of her work, came across a lovely little orphan girl. She asked me if I would take her in. I agreed to take her into my family. After completing all formalities, she became the first child. A few days later another child was brought who also needed to be looked after. It was then that the idea of starting an orphanage came to me.

Gradually, over the years, the number increased to four and an orphanage was started with these children at 34, Elgin Road. Later, by 1979, the number of babies increased to twelve.

At this stage, the orphanage was named Kamal Kanan and was brought under the banner of the Julien Charitable and Educational Trust, with twelve children between the ages of three days and two years.

For this purpose a building was purchased in Ganganagar. The children were moved from Elgin Road to Ganganagar where they lived as a big family and grew up.

Schooling was at the adjoining Julien Day School. They did not fare too well under the ICSE pattern, so I approached Ms Chaya Biswas, principal of St Thomas' Girls' School, Kidderpore, to prepare them for the Open School exams of classes X and XII. It was very kind of her to take them in without hesitation. They were also admitted into the hostel. I used to make weekly trips to go and see them. One of them went further in her education. I got her admitted in Loreto House where she graduated successfully in English Honours. Now they are all grown up, married and have children of their own.

Sheila Broughton epitomizes the best qualities of a teacher and educationist—deeply committed, compassionate and most of all, with a steely determination that has seen her overcome all manner of obstacles in her work. Every child whose life she has touched will remember her with affection and gratitude.

PHILOMENA EATON

Philomena Eaton is a visionary brimming with solicitude for her fellow beings. She was one of the best professional secretaries of her time, and worked tirelessly to improve the conditions and image of others in the profession. Later, she dedicated all her time and energy for the less fortunate Anglo-Indians in Kolkata.

The Anglo-Indian lady secretary was once the hallmark of perhaps every noteworthy commercial organization, particularly in Kolkata. Efficient, trustworthy and smartly turned out, the Anglo-Indian girl was a vital cog in the working of an establishment.

Eaton was one of them. She completed her secretarial course after passing the Pitman's Institute examination.

A Kolkata girl, the lure of the open spaces drew her to Assam in 1960, where she worked as a secretary to the Assam Oil Company for three years and was then transferred as secretary to the Managing Director of the newly opened oilfields at Duliajan.

In1963, Philomena returned to Kolkata to look after her ailing mother, since two siblings had gotten married and left home and a brother had joined the Jesuit seminary. She then continued to work at various tea estates and at leading firms like HSBC. For twenty years, she worked for the Managing

Director of Jokai India which owned twelve tea gardens in Assam (later the company was renamed Rossell Industries Ltd).

At a time when her life was a busy whirl of work and holidays spent swimming and playing tennis, Eaton felt an emptiness take hold within her. There was something lacking in her life, she felt, and she joined the Legion of Mary, a church organization where she served as President and Secretary for many years. It is here that she first started reaching out to the lonely, neglected and unwanted.

Her work with the organization provided new enthusiasm and drive into her life and her workplace and life in general became more interesting. She found that social service and working as a secretary complemented each other.

She now decided that professional secretaries needed an organization of their own to address their concerns and to best train themselves for the future. The National Institute of Professional Secretaries (NIPS) was her next venture, and she joined as one of its founder members. The organization helped secretaries through frequent lecture sessions and communication courses.

On 14 March 1987, the first All-India Secretary of the Year contest was held in Mumbai. It was a landmark moment in the history of the secretarial profession in India. The grandeur of the famous Taj Mahal Hotel ballroom provided an appropriate setting for the occasion when over 500 guests assembled to accord recognition and to applaud the best of India's lady secretaries.

The contestants were judged for charm, poise, intelligence, and most importantly, professional excellence. At the final stage of the selection process, each finalist was interviewed by a panel of judges, just as though she was being considered for the post of a personal secretary. The finalists were also asked to speak extempore for two minutes on a topic given to them only minutes before they stepped on to the podium. Philomena's topic was: 'How to handle a difficult boss'! Needless to say, Philomena Eaton was declared India's first Secretary of the Year.

Meanwhile, Eaton's work in the social services was becoming more and more important for her. She was a founder member of the Calcutta Anglo-Indian Service Society (CAISS) in 1976. The organization recognized the poor economic conditions of certain sections of Anglo-Indians and over the years, it has been involved in meeting the needs of the poorer sections of the community. It helps around 250 senior citizens by providing assistance in the form of rations, medicines and a monthly pension. It helps the children of the community by taking care of their school fees, books, boarding fees, uniform, 'tiffin' and transport expenses. CAISS also assists Anglo-Indians in finding suitable jobs, and its self-employment panel trains women in sewing, embroidery and knitting.

CAISS is a member of the International Federation of Anglo-Indian Organizations, and was awarded the right to host the IXth Anglo-Indian Reunion in Kolkata from January 6 to 12, 2013.

Spearheading all these activities is the strong-willed and ever-energetic Convenor of CAISS, Philomena Eaton. She is one of the leading lights of the community today, a person with a unique vision of life where she sees the human potential around her, and works tirelessly for the common good.

'There is no greater religion than human service' sums up Philomena Eaton's motto in life.

—Errol O'Brien

∾

THE SCHOLAR AND MENTOR

Neil O'Brien (1934–)

'Who or what is thurifer?' It's been some forty years since the quizmaster asked the question but Jug Suraiya, journalist, writer and, in an age and a Calcutta gone by, an avid quizzer, can remember it as if it were yesterday.

It was clear soon enough that nobody had the answer. The expressions on the team members' faces told the story. It was then that the participants and the audience, and most acutely Jug, saw a virtuoso performance. Neil O'Brien attempted to fudge the answer.

To a practised quizzer, fudging is not an artifice; it is an art form. It is to start the process of answering a question with a clue, a ghost of a clue or sometimes not even that—and to negotiate with and draw out information from the quizmaster that leads him to give the game away. No one did it better than Neil O'Brien.

'Neil began waving his hands,' Jug remembers, 'as if he were performing some intricate dance *mudra*s. "A thurifer," he said, "is a is a is a…"

"Is a…?" The quizmaster was getting impatient.

"In religious ceremonies…" Neil mumbled.

"What about religious ceremonies?" The quizmaster stopped in his tracks. Neil had him captive. The first round had been won.

"In Christian religious ceremonies…" Neil continued, doing nothing more than giving himself time, and watching the quizmaster's face as if to decode it.

"Go on," went the quizmaster, by now confused if Neil knew the answer or whether he should put a stop to this and move to the next team.

"You know the thing with incense…"

"The thing?" The quizmaster was about to pass, but for one transfixing moment Neil looked him in the eye.

'Then came the flourish. With a masterful wave of the hands Neil O'Brien had the answer: "Not *thing*, he… It's the person, the person who carries the incense during worship in church."

'The quizmaster nodded, Neil and his team had the point.'

Jug was left not just impressed but bewildered. It was almost magical; Neil had plucked an answer out of thin air.

Later the two friends got talking. Neil confessed he had known nothing of the definition of 'thurifer'. Shortly after the question was asked, he vaguely remembered the vessel used to burn incense in church was called a thurible. Could the two words be linked? He had started off with just that surmise, finally getting his answer when the quizmaster emphasized the word 'thing', indicating, to the watchful, that he was seeking not an object but an animate being.

Jug counts Neil as among his closest and oldest friends. To

him, that episode, that fudging expedition at a quiz and that answer remain emblematic of Neil. 'He is a man of erudition,' Jug says fondly, 'but also practical common sense, and the ability to make connections.' He has the empathy, Jug says, to read clues offered in the expressions or mannerisms of another human being. Above all, he is a hard customer, a keen competitor who will fight for that answer and that point till the very end, even resorting to some intellectual gamesmanship if necessary.

∾

Jug Suraiya's anecdote about Neil—or Neil Aloysius O'Brien to give him his full name—reflects the mosaic that makes up the man. His quest to learn, to study, to seek the frontiers of knowledge; his determination to reach the identifiable goals of a successful career; his competitive edge, the result of childhood insecurities perhaps, that have sublimated themselves in the most agreeable of battlegrounds—the quiz: this is at once a simple and a complex man.

Maybe he represents his rich and mixed ancestry. It would have confused a lesser person, but for Neil it is a matter of honour and a badge of pride. 'I'm Anglo-Indian,' he often says, 'as proud of the Anglo or European side of my heritage as the Indian side.'

There is somewhere in him a bit of the hardy, adventurous Thomas O'Brien, an Irish soldier who came to India shortly after the Mutiny, fought and won a medal in the Bhutan War of 1864-'65 and never went home. There is also somewhere in Neil more than a bit of Nellie Bella O'Brien, his upstanding and redoubtable grandmother, born to a Bengali Christian family, married to Thomas' son Daniel in 1904—the bride was fifteen, the groom in his thirties—and widowed early. Left to bring up her children on her own, Nellie first educated herself—becoming among Bengal's earliest women doctors—and then her children. Her greatest, most rewarding mission was nurturing her grandson, Neil, who was left in her care after his parents separated in the 1940s.

Nellie left a deep impact on Neil. The medal she won at Calcutta Medical College is still one of his prized possessions. With him too are memories of a childhood that now seems so far away. He was born to Edna and Amos in 1934, being delivered at home by his grandmother. This was around the time Nellie gave up her job in a Jalpaiguri hospital to return to Calcutta and set up a private practice. They didn't know it then, but it was to forge a bond between grandmother and grandson that only grew stronger as the years passed.

When World War II broke out, there were fears of a Japanese invasion or bombing of Calcutta. Neil and his grandmother were sent off in 1940 and then 1942 to Peshawar, where Amos's brother Patrick was a civil servant. 'I remember a holiday in Nathiagali, close to Abbottabad,' Neil says, 'it was the summering station of the Governor of the North-West Frontier... One of my earliest holidays.' There was also a short stint in a school in Agra: 'I had to learn Urdu but wrote it the wrong way, and got zero. But I came first in English!'

It was in Calcutta, however, that Neil walked down the road of formal education, beginning with Loreto Convent in Sealdah—it still took boys back then—before moving in class II to St Xavier's, so close to his first home on Park Lane, just off Park Street. Soon he was living in the Jamir Lane house that is still the O'Brien home. His father had left to teach at a college in Kerala—Amos subsequently became the first Christian to serve as head of the Department of English, Banaras Hindu University, and also taught at Cuttack's Ravenshaw College—and it was Nellie who brought up little Neil.

By his own admission, Neil was a shy and lonely boy. At St Xavier's, it was a Belgian Jesuit, Father John Biot, who drew him out of his shell. 'He touched my life,' Neil says, expressing an emotion that, despite the length of time, cannot hide gratitude. 'I began to open up. He got me interested in sport, football, hockey and dramatics. The Kendals came to Calcutta and performed at Xavier's. I saw every single play. My exposure to Shakespeare was not through books but because I saw his plays being performed...'

This was the trigger the inquisitive and intellectually agile lad needed. Neil was academically proficient. Those who marvel at his ability to identify and decipher obscure Latin phrases—attributes that have served him in several quizzes—would be interested to know he studied and topped Latin in school. 'It helped me with my knowledge of and curiosity for the English language,' he says. Higher education was a natural progression. Neil hopped across to St Xavier's College, exploring the world of music and theatre, becoming sociable, 'and also began to go to church daily with my grandmother'. The boy was becoming a man: 'But I was still a shy chap. No girlfriends!'

∼

In the 1950s, jobs were reserved for Anglo-Indians in government departments that had a tradition of service by the community—the Railways, the Customs and Calcutta Police. After school and certainly after college, many of Neil's Anglo-Indian friends took up jobs. 'I was envious of them and their uniforms and motorcycles, he admits, 'but I plodded along for an MA.' Encouraged by his grandmother who saw academic potential in him, he went to Calcutta University, saw a different side to his city and society, and even got elected class representative in Students' Union elections.

It was in his final year as an MA student that Neil had two life-altering experiences. First, at a party at a common friend's house on Theatre Road, he met Joyce. 'It was love at first sight'—after all these years, he remains as definitive as ever. Joyce was the antithesis of Neil. Cheerful, gregarious and extroverted, she was born to a large happy Railway family of ten children. She had lived all over India—in modern Maharashtra and Andhra Pradesh, Bihar and Bengal. On a family holiday years later—the O'Briens were driving from Calcutta to Madras (Kolkata to Chennai in today's parlance)—she stunned village folk at the Orissa-Andhra border by addressing them in Telugu.

Neil's and Joyce's personalities complemented each other. As they went their separate ways that evening after the party, they promised to stay in touch. Pretty soon, it was clear they were serious about each other. Joyce moved to Calcutta to her uncle's house and began teaching at South Point school. In 1959, at Christ the King Church, Calcutta, the two were married.

Before that Neil had found his calling—publishing. In 1956, he joined Longman as a trainee. 'In the morning, I edited,' he says of his early days at work, 'and in the afternoons, I was taken on sales calls, to the warehouse and other departments. It was a thorough grounding in all aspects of the publishing business. Only after two years did I get an executive post.'

It was not an easy life. To supplement his income, Neil took tuitions in the evening and taught English and commercial correspondence to B.Com students at St Xavier's between 6 a.m. and 8 a.m. 'Often I'd be home only for dinner,' he says. 'It was tough… but it was also strange to see that among my students were friends who had joined the Customs straight after school. They had now come back because they needed a college degree to get promoted.' By 1961, the job quotas had gone. Neil's focus on education had paid off.

In 1965, Neil joined Oxford University Press (OUP) as manager of its Calcutta office. He did a short stint in New Delhi in the early 1970s, before returning to Calcutta. In the 1990s, he went back to the capital, retiring as Managing Director of OUP in 1996. Anglo-Indians have made it to the top of the armed forces, but Neil was perhaps the first from the community to head a major private sector company. Indeed, many would see in him the very model for a young Anglo-Indian.

Even so, in the forty years he spent in publishing, Neil saw many Anglo-Indians leave India—for Britain, Canada, America, Australia. It was often an instinctive and emotional decision, rather than based on a thought-out economic strategy. 'I think they got overwhelmed by the idea of having to work for "Indians",' Neil says, obviously regretful. 'I know two brothers, one of them stayed on and became a successful police officer. The other was a former army man and perhaps better qualified, but he left. And lived in oblivion in England. He gave up a comfortable life in India for almost nothing.'

It was not an option Neil even thought of exercising. 'I never considered leaving,' he says. 'I had to fit into the new India, I was determined. In Jamir Lane, I began to learn the language of my neighbours without studying it formally. I wanted to be a local boy.' In part this was his grandmother's influence. In part it was Joyce's influence; with her pan-Indian background, in terms of where she'd stayed, this was the only country she could call home.

The impulse to speak Bengali, to mingle with the rest of the city and not stand out as different—Neil and Joyce (and Nellie) passed this on to the next generation. At an inter-company football match on the Maidan in the 1980s, Andy, Neil's second son, was sledged in Bengali and surprised his opponent by giving it right back in even more colourful Bengali.

Andy was a well-regarded and award-winning sports journalist before moving to Australia, where he works at the Department of Education in Perth. Of his brothers, Barry followed in the footsteps of his grandfather and father and made a career as a teacher and an educationist, teaching for a while in South Point, where his mother too had taught. Barry also succeeded his father as an MLA from the Anglo-Indian community. On his part, Derek, now an MP in the Rajya Sabha, made a business of quizzing and the enterprise of knowledge.

Writing and publishing, education, a thirst for knowledge and learning, quizzing, public service: each of Neil's sons has inherited and optimised a facet of his father. The unit has been held together, however, by the remarkably non-judgemental Joyce—the sheet-anchor of the family.

Joyce and Neil have grown up and grown old together; they have seen the world together, including during an unforgettable round-the-world trip that was Neil's farewell gift from OUP. An early overseas visit took place in 1966, when OUP summoned Neil for six weeks to England and when he travelled to a business event in Germany.

The young couple, familiar with many of the cultural

reference points of London—which self-respecting Calcuttan of that era wasn't!—had a ball. They watched theatre and sport and television. Something caught Neil's eye: the quiz shows. 'We saw many quizzes on television,' he recalls, 'and I was hooked. It struck me that participants of Indian ethnicity— and there were a few even back then—seemed to have the answers.'

In December 1967, Neil conducted Calcutta's first open quiz at the Parish Club adjoining Christ the King Church. 'A former President had died and we wanted to organize an event in his honour,' he says. 'I suggested a quiz.' There were only five teams, but a snowball had started rolling. In the years to follow, Neil's stewardship of the Dalhousie Institute A or DI (A) team made it one of the most formidable quartets on Calcutta's open quiz circuit. It led to younger and sometimes awe-struck quizzers giving him the sobriquet 'The Man Who Knows Everything'.

Ten years later, Neil began taking part in a Question Hour of quite another kind, in the West Bengal legislative assembly. Till then far away from politics, and even community politics, he was astounded when he called home one day from his hotel in Madras (Chennai). His flight had been delayed and he didn't want Joyce to worry. She said some of his friends had been asking for him and Jyoti Basu, newly-elected Chief Minister of the state, wanted to meet him. Basu, a fellow Xaverian, had sought out Neil and wanted him to accept the nomination as Anglo-Indian MLA.

Initially hesitant, Neil took to his quasi-political office with his trademark honesty of purpose. Since he held a full-time job, any advance in his community leadership role was possible only if Joyce took half the burden. She did so willingly and became actively involved in the All-India Anglo-Indian Association, making herself a bridge between the community and its MLA.

Neil, who was to serve three terms before stepping down in 1991, realized he needed to talk to ordinary folks in the community, not just his friends, much more often and with much more patience. 'Every Monday, Wednesday and Friday,' he says, 'after work at OUP, I would go to St Mary's on Ripon Street and just sit there and meet people. They poured in, with problems of marriages, police cases, landlord evictions. I saw Anglo-Indians at their best, and I saw them at their worst.'

It was only a matter of time before Neil began to be spoken of as a prospective Anglo-Indian MP (two members of the community are nominated to the Lok Sabha or Lower House of India's Parliament). In 1991, the lawyer Frank Anthony, a long-standing MP and doyen of the community, sounded him out for the position. 'I sought permission from OUP, but they said no,' Neil explains. Unwilling to give up his chance to head OUP in India, and reach the peak of his professional career, Neil turned down the offer. In 1997, shortly after he retired from the company, Indrajit Gupta, an old friend and then India's Home Minister, asked Neil again. This time he was ready.

In the interim, in 1993, Frank Anthony had died and Neil soon donned his mantle as senior statesman of the Anglo-Indian community. He became President-in-Chief of the All-India Anglo-Indian Association, the oldest and only pan-Indian Anglo-Indian organization in the country, a position he continues to hold today. He also heads the Frank Anthony Schools in Delhi, Kolkata and Bangalore. Just after Frank Anthony's death, Neil took his place as Chairman of the Council for the Indian School Certificate Examinations, the authority to which many premier schools in the country are affiliated and which derives from the old Senior Cambridge regime. He held this prestigious office for two decades. This completed the circle and brought him back to the academic domain that had reared him. He stepped down from his leadership of the Council in 2010, insisting it was time to retire and relax with the grandchildren.

Alas, this time he wasn't fudging.

—ASHOK MALIK

THE WRITER ON THE HILL

Ruskin Bond (1934–)

I had a brief but memorable encounter with Ruskin Bond when he was on one of his rare visits to Kolkata some time in 2003. He had left the hills for a few days and had come down to Kolkata to pray by his father's grave at the Bhawanipur Cemetery. He was lodged in the guest rooms of the Faraway Pavilions at the Tollygunge Club, where I met him along with a bunch of enthusiastic teen reporters for a weekly students' paper.

The quiet, self-effacing author opened up in the company of the excited teenagers, and regaled us with many witticisms.

'Remember Sean Connery as 007?' he said. 'He stylishly introduced himself as "I'm Bond. James Bond." Well,' quipped Ruskin, 'I'm the original Bond.'

For over forty years he has lived in the little hill town of Mussoorie. When we asked why, he replied, 'I forgot to go away!' Then he added, 'That's partly true. I have had good times here as well as bad times but the good times have dominated. There's something to be said for a place if you have been happy there.

It is nice to record some of the events that have made up fun and happy living.'

Bond has written extensively about his life as a writer, and for me to add anything to that would be like showing a candle to the wind. Hence, I thought it best to reproduce here a piece he wrote about living in the mountains, about why he has never lived anywhere else, and about his extended adopted family.

—Editor

The Writer on the Hill

It's hard to realize that I've been here all these years—forty summers and monsoons and winters and Himalayan springs—because, when I look back to the time of my first coming here, it really does seem like yesterday.

That probably sums it all up. Time passes, and yet it doesn't pass (it is only you and I who are passing). People come and go, the mountains remain. Mountains are permanent things. They are stubborn, they refuse to move. You can blast holes out of them for their mineral wealth; or strip them of their trees and foliage; or dam their streams and divert their torrents; or make tunnels and roads and bridges; but no matter how hard they try, humans cannot actually get rid of these mountains. That's what I like about them; they are here to stay.

I like to think that I have become a part of this mountain, this particular range, and that by living here for so long, I am able to claim a relationship with the trees, wild flowers, even the rocks that are an integral part of it. Yesterday, at twilight, when I passed beneath the canopy of oak leaves, I felt that I was a part of the forest. I put out my hand and touched the bark of an old tree and as I turned away, its leaves brushed against my face as if to acknowledge me.

One day I thought, if we trouble these great creatures too much, and hack away at them and destroy their young, they will simply uproot themselves and march away—whole forests on the move—over the next range and the next, far from the haunts of man. Over the years, I have seen many forests and green places dwindle and disappear.

Now there is an outcry. It is suddenly fashionable to be an environmentalist. That's all right. Perhaps it isn't too late to save the little that's left. They could start by curbing the property developers, who have been spreading their tentacles far and wide.

The sea has been celebrated by many great writers— Conrad, Melville, Stevenson, Masefield—but I cannot think of anyone comparable for whom the mountains have been a recurring theme. I must turn to the Taoist poets from old China to find a true feeling for mountains. Kipling does occasionally look to the hills, but the Himalayas do not appear to have given rise to any memorable Indian literature, at least not in modern times.

By and large, I suppose, writers have to stay in the plains to make a living. Hill people have their work cut out just to wrest a livelihood from their thin, calcinated soil. And as for mountaineers, they climb their peaks and move on, in search of other peaks; they do not take up residence in the mountains.

But to me, as a writer, the mountains have been kind. They were kind from the beginning, when I threw up a job in Delhi and rented a small cottage on the outskirts of the hill-station. Today, most hill-stations are rich men's playgrounds, but twenty-five years ago, they were places where people of modest means could live quite cheaply. There were very few cars and everyone walked about.

The cottage was situated on the edge of an oak and maple forest and I spent eight or nine years in it, most of them happy years, writing stories, essays, poems, books for children. It was only after I came to live in the hills that I began writing for children.

I think this had something to do with Prem's children. Prem Singh came to work for me as a boy, fresh from his village near Rudraprayag, in Pauri Garhwal. He was taller and darker than most of the young men from his area. Although in those days the village school did not go beyond the primary stage, he had an aptitude for reading and a good head for figures.

After he had been with me for a couple of years, he went home to get married, and then he and his wife Chandra took on the job of looking after the house and all practical matters; I remain helpless with electric-fuses, clogged cisterns, leaking gas cylinders, ruptured water pipes, tin roofs that blow away whenever there is a storm, and the do-it-yourself world of hill-station India. In other words, they made it possible for a writer to write.

They also nursed me when I was ill, and gave me a feeling of belonging to a family, something which I hadn't known since childhood.

Their sons Rakesh and Mukesh, and daughter Savitri, grew up in Maplewood Cottage and then in other houses and cottages where we moved. I became, for them, an adopted grandfather. For Rakesh, I wrote a story about a cherry tree that had difficulty in growing up (he was rather frail as a child). For Mukesh, who liked upheavals, I wrote a story about an earthquake and put him in it; and for Savitri I wrote a whole bunch of rhymes and poems.

One seldom ran short of material. There was a stream at the bottom of the hill and this gave me many subjects in the way of small (occasionally large) animals, wild flowers, birds, trees, insects, ferns. The nearby villages were of absorbing interest. So were the old houses and old families of the Landour and Mussoorie hill-stations.

There were walks into the mountains and along the pilgrim trails, and sometimes I slept at a roadside tea-shop or at a village school. Sadly, many of these villages are still without basic medical and educational facilities that are taken for granted elsewhere.

'Who goes to the hills, goes to his mother.' So wrote Kipling in *Kim* and he seldom wrote truer words, for living in the hills was like living in the bosom of a strong, sometimes proud, but always comforting, mother. And every time I went away, the homecoming would be more tender and precious. It became increasingly difficult for me to go away. Once the mountains are in your blood, there is no escape.

It has not always been happiness and light. Two-year-old Suresh (who came between Rakesh and Mukesh) died of tetanus. I had bouts of ill-health, and there were times when money ran out. Freelancing can be daunting at times, and I never could make enough to buy a house like almost everyone else I know.

Editorial doors close; but when one door closes, another has, for me almost immediately, miraculously opened. I could perhaps have done a little better living in London or Hong Kong, or even in Bombay. But given the choice, I would not have done differently. When you have received love from people and freedom only the mountains can give, you have come very near the borders of heaven.

And now, Rakesh and Beena have three lovely children, and Mukesh and Vinita have two little scamps.

—RUSKIN BOND

From *All Roads Lead to Ganga* (Rupa Publications India Pvt. Ltd., 2007)

SABRE JET DOWN

Trevor Keelor (1934-2002)

Stories of war heroes have often been the main inspiration for many young persons to join the defence forces. The fierce desire to prove oneself in the face of overwhelming odds, to never accept defeat, are the hallmarks of the stories of people like Douglas Bader and of accounts like *The Dam Busters.* Bader was a Royal Air Force (RAF) pilot who continued to fly despite being an amputee. *The Dam Busters* is the account of RAF Squadron 617 which used specially designed bombs in order to destroy the Ruhr dams of Germany.

Like many of our generation, the Keelor brothers of Lucknow—Denzil and Trevor—were also deeply inspired by these stories, as well as by people like Winston Churchill and his leadership of Britain during World War II. The brothers became household names in India for their daring raids deep into Pakistani territory as pilots of the Indian Air Force Gnat planes during the India-Pakistan war of 1965. The war took place between the months of April and September of that year, and it saw the largest massing of troops in Kashmir since the Partition. Infantry battalions and armoured vehicles were backed by Air Force and naval units.

The Keelors were the first brothers to receive the Vir Chakra for the same feat—the shooting down of Sabre jets. This article is about one of the brothers, Wing Commander Trevor Keelor.

Keelor was born in Lucknow and educated in St George's College, Mussoorie, and St Francis' College, Lucknow. He joined the Indian Air Force in 1953 and displayed great presence of mind in critical situations right from the start.

He was awarded the Vayu Sena Medal in 1964. His citation says that on 5 February 1964, he had to ferry a Gnat from Poona to Palam in a squadron formation of five aircraft. The last part of the flight had to be taken at 41,000 feet. While descending to land at Palam, he was alarmed to discover that there was no response from the engine to the throttle movements. The Gnats already had a reputation of crashes and fatal landings and realizing the danger of the situation, Keelor broke off from the formation and with great presence of mind and careful handling, he accomplished the forced landing successfully without any damage to the aircraft.

What were these Gnat aircraft that Keelor became so adept at handling? Let me attempt to describe.

The Gnat fighter aircraft were designed in the United Kingdom. In India, they were constructed by Hindustan Aeronautics Ltd, Bangalore. The designers' brief was to create an aircraft that would be the smallest possible in size, and yet be effective in a dog fight. The speed of the Gnat could reach 688 mph. It could carry 240 gallons of fuel internally and 40 gallons in two underwings jettisionable tanks.

They were designed to be so small that it would be difficult to spot them on the radar screen. They were also very manoeuverable. For fighters, the most important factor is turning a full circle. The aircraft had a small turning radius. But the Gnat also had many technical problems. Test pilots flying Gnats were lost in accidents. The Keelor brothers, however, were experts at flying the Gnat and used it to shoot down the larger and superior Sabre Jets used by the Pakistan Air Force.

The first victory of the Indian Air force in aerial combat against the Pakistan Air Force was provided by Trevor Keelor. He was awarded the Vir Chakra for displaying courage and leadership

This is what his citation says:

On 3rd September 1965, on receipt of a report that a formation of Pakistani fighters were circling over our Army position in the Chhamb Sector of J&K, a formation of Gnat aircraft was ordered to intercept the intruders. Approaching the area, Sqn Ldr Trevor Keelor, who was a section leader in the Gnat formation, sighted enemy F-86 Sabre jets and engaged them in air battle. When the combat was in progress, F-104 Starfighters of the Pakistan Air Force also joined in. Unmindful of the numerical superiority of the enemy, Sqn Ldr Keelor chased a Sabre jet and pressed home his attack until the enemy aircraft caught fire and disintegrated in the air. This was the first victory of our Air Force in the air battles against the Pakistan Air Force. In this operation, Sqn Ldr Keelor displayed courage and leadership of a high order in the best traditions of the Air Force.

His elder brother, Denzil Keelor, who also received the Vir Chakra for a similar feat received this citation:

> On 19th September 1965, Sqn Ldr Denzil Keelor was providing fighter escort to Mystere aircraft during a strike mission in the operations against Pakistan. His section of four Gnat aircraft was engaged by four enemy Sabre jet aircraft and the battle was fought at a height of less than 2,000 feet from the ground where enemy anti-aircraft guns were also active. Under his guidance, his subsection leader shot down a Sabre jet aircraft. Thereafter Sqn Ldr Keelor himself engaged another Sabre jet and crippled it. Throughout the operations, Sqn Ldr Keelor was a source of inspiration to his pilots and ground personnel. His courage and devotion to duty were in the best traditions of the Air Force.

The courageous feats of these brothers have provided inspiration to countless Anglo-Indian youngsters, leading many to join the armed forces and distinguishing themselves in the service of the country.

—Errol O'Brien

OF A THOUSAND AND ONE DANCES

Helen Richardson (1939–)

Deep in the ravines, Gabbar Singh, the most feared outlaw in India, is meeting his arms dealer. The heroes are laying dynamite fuses to blow up his stash of arms. Around the bonfire, a gypsy strikes a note, and a shimmering dancer emerges. She is on screen for all of four minutes, the duration of what will become the iconic 'Mehbooba' song. Yet, the impact of that one dance number on every member of the audience, even twenty-five years later, is one of open-mouthed wonder.

That's Helen for you. If there was one person who epitomized the cliché 'setting the screen on fire', it is Helen Richardson, actor and dancer, who has appeared in over 700 Hindi films in a career spanning from 1951 (*Awaara*) to 2000 (*Mohabbatein*).

I recall when I spoke to Helen, and explained to her that I was doing this piece on her, she exclaimed, 'Yes, if you consider me to be Anglo-Indian, I would be very happy to be in the book, though honestly, I have never consciously thought of myself as one... I have never lived life in the typical Anglo-Indian way...'

Helen's life story is no less dramatic than some of the roles she acted out on screen. Born to an Anglo-Indian father and a Burmese mother, she lost her father on the battlefront during World War II. Burma was at the time under Japanese attack and mass evacuations were underway. Desperate for survival, her mother fled with three-year-old Helen and her baby brother. Unable to find a flight out of Burma as the aerodrome was bombed to smithereens, the family joined the hundreds of refugee families on a long trek over the Arakan mountains and through the forests of Assam.

Hungry and weary they trekked on, occasionally being offered food by villagers on the way. They were also helped by British soldiers who passed the refugee columns. They finally reached Dibrugarh in Assam. By then Helen was reduced to a skeleton and had to spend two months recovering in a hospital.

The family then moved to Kolkata, where her mother worked as a nurse. But tragedy struck them again. Helen's little brother died of small pox. Devastated, mother and daughter now moved to Hyderabad and then to Deolali in northern Maharashtra. Finally, they found their way to Mumbai in 1945.

Helen's mother got to know some people in the Hindi movie industry, and decided on a career for her little girl. Helen was going to be a dancer. So while her friends were out playing, Helen had to learn how to dance under the strict supervision of her mother.

At the time, a dancer named Cuckoo was very popular. Helen came to her notice and she took the talented young girl under her wing. Though it was poverty that threw her into the world of Hindi films, it is also true that Helen loved dancing and her gift could not have gone unnoticed for long.

Dinesh Rajah and Jitendra Kothari in *The Hundred Luminaries of Hindi Cinema* describe Helen as: 'A slit-eyed teenage girl of Spanish and Burmese ancestry who arrived in Bombay having escaped from Burma. The legs that carried her through the jungles of the North-East were later to take her to fame.'

Helen started off as one of the backup dancers and got her first opportunity in films like *Shabistan* and *Awaara* in 1951. But it was her mischievous and endearing turn in the song 'Mera Naam Chin Chin Chu' in *Howrah Bridge* that set her on the path of dancing glory.

In the 1960s, Hindi film music saw a change in rhythm, pace and style. Faster beats, Western tunes and less inhibited dance numbers became popular. In this decade, Helen truly explored her skills as a dancer and actor. As Jerry Pinto says in his book on Helen, she exploded on to the scene like an H-Bomb. Her physical energy and charm captivated audiences. She was a pin-up girl, yet strangely there was never anything cheap about her moves. They were sensual with a tinge of innocence.

Helen's dancing style was a blend of the Indian and Western. She could perform the cabaret or the flamenco with equal ease without losing the particularly Indian touch and expressions.

Helen also acted in a number of movies in the 1960s and 1970s, most notably in *Jewel Thief* (1967) and *Gumnaam* (1965) for which she received a Filmfare nomination for Best Supporting Actress.

In 1981, Helen married screenwriter Salim Khan and slowly moved away from the film world. In later years she has done short but impactful roles in movies like *Khamoshi: The Musical* (1996), *Hum Dil De Chuke Sanam* (1999) and *Mohabbatein* (2000). In the last, the jaws of the audience dropped once more when she swiftly cast aside her prim headmistress persona to do an energetic jive on the dance floor. Clearly, the energy and charisma were still intact!

Helen has fascinated generations of film lovers and writers on cinema. A documentary called *Helen: Queen of the Nautch Girls* was made by Merchant Ivory Films in 1973.

Jerry Pinto's book, *Helen: The Life and Times of an H-Bomb* (2006) was a study written of the complex space Helen has occupied in the Hindi film world by a professed fan. The book won the National Film Award for the Best Book on Cinema in 2007.

Helen has received a number of accolades. She won the Filmfare Award for Best Supporting Actress for *Lahu Ke Do Rang* in 1979, and the Filmfare Lifetime Achievement Award in 1998. In 2000, she was awarded the Padma Shri.

It's been an eventful life for this dancing queen, and she has lit up the lives of countless fans along the way!

—Andrew Scolt

JAGUARS CAN FLY

Michael McMahon (1944–)

'In most activities in our daily lives, one can make some mistakes, make the corrections, say sorry, and move on; but there are some professions in the world where such a luxury is not available.

A fighter pilot is part of such a profession that whenever the minutest mistake occurs, it can lead to tragedy.'

—Air Marshal Michael McMahon (Retd.)

In full uniform, his achievements and decorations should have weighed him down:

Awarded Param Vishisht Seva Medal in Jan 2002
Ati Vishisht Seva Medal in Jan 1997
Vayu Sena Medal in Jan 1980

But nothing could weigh Michael McMahon down. Not then not now.

Despite a scroll of credits to his name, for his colleagues in the Indian Air Force, McMahon's greatest achievement was his constant adherence to the highest standards of professional and personal conduct.

This sense of honour was evident even on the very last day of his service in 2004. He vacated his office and official residence within hours of his retirement so that his successor could quickly move in. He retired as Vice Chief of Air Staff, the number two spot in the Indian Air Force—the service he had served with dedication and honour for several decades.

This philosophy of 'trusting in God and doing the right thing' in all circumstances was ingrained in the four McMahon boys from an early age, when they were growing up in the Kidderpore area of Kolkata. McMahon completed his education at Sherwood School in Naini Tal, also the alma mater of Field Marshal Sam Manekshaw.

He was commissioned as a fighter pilot in the Indian Air Force on the 22 June 1963, standing first in flying within his batch. He went on to become one of the youngest to face a war mission in 1965 and flew out in the Chhamb sector after the infiltration of Pakistani troops.

Again in 1971, when India and Pakistan were at war, McMahon was one of the officers called upon to protect Indian air space.

In both these conflicts, he was Mentioned in Dispatches. A soldier Mentioned in Dispatches is one whose name appears in an official report written by a superior officer and sent to the high command, in which the soldier's gallant or meritorious action in the face of enemy action is described.

In 1999, when the hostilities broke out at Kargil, as the

Senior Air Staff Officer at Western Air Command, he was responsible for the conduct of air operations in Kargil. It was a highly successful air battle that led to the early culmination of the war.

Earlier in his career, Michael McMahon was in the first batch of pilots to be trained to fly Jaguars in the UK. After leading the team that flew in the Jaguars to India he later commanded two Jaguar squadrons. Subsequently, he also commanded Air Force Station, Ambala—India's premier fighter base.

McMahon was part of the 2221st Tiger Squadron who flew Sabre jets with the United States Air Force. He also underwent training with various aircraft in advanced gunnery courses in the USA.

In 1967, he was part of the first batch selected to train in Russia on the Sukhoi-7 and help in its seamless induction into the IAF.

McMahon was always passionate about training other pilots. He became a qualified flying instructor and was the winner of the Air Chief's Trophy for standing first in flying.

In the 1970s, he twice served on the staff at the IAF's Tactics and Combat Development and Training Establishment. As a result of his qualifications, he was deputed for two years to the Government of Iraq as a flying instructor. He also served as Director of Air Staff Requirements and Assistant Chief of Air Staff (Operations). In 1985, he underwent Joint Services' Staff College Course from the Joint Services' Staff College in Canberra, Australia. Such a course helps educate officers in the nuances of staff work which is required for postings at Air or Command Headquarters.

In early 2001, McMahon was the Inspector General of the

IAF and then the AOC in C of South Western Air Command from August 2001 to February 2003. The period spanned the thirteen months of Operation Parakram when, after the attack on the Indian Parliament, the defence forces were deployed and kept in constant readiness on the western borders of the country.

McMahon retired as the Vice Chief of the Air Staff after forty-two years of service.

He now lives in Bangalore with his wife Linda.

In fact Linda is the great love and romance of Michael McMahon's life. His mother Phyllis loved a game of weekend tennis on the courts of the Dalhousie Institute in Kolkata and was also part of the club quiz team. Linda and her mother, Gloria, were tennis addicts as well, though Linda also represented her school in basketball and even made the national team.

Romance blossomed on the lawns of the Dalhousie Institute, and Michael and Linda got married in 1970. They have two remarkable sons who have chosen their professions overseas.

Always the family man, when I spoke to him about his many achievements, McMahon said, 'You must not forget to mention that my grandson, Mark, received his first swimming certificate just after he was a year old! That is a far greater achievement than any of mine. Also, my wife is a professional home-maker and by far the best cook in the world!'

McMahon's brothers, Keith, Brian and David, live in Australia, but due to the choice of his profession, McMahon did not have the flexibility to leave and settle in another country as so many Anglo-Indians did.

In all the flying he learnt and excelled in, there was one

kind of flight Michael McMahon never learnt: how to fly the nest. And India is indebted to him for this.

—Errol O'Brien

Only one Anglo-Indian has risen to the position of Chief of Air Staff of the Indian Air Force, and that is Air Chief Marshal Denis Anthony La Fontaine (1929–2011). I had just established contact with him in order to record his life story, when he passed away in April 2011. My conversation with him remained unfinished, and this book the poorer without a full profile of this remarkable Air Force man. I salute him nonetheless for being a true pathbreaker from the community.

—Editor

THE ALFORD FAMILY

This is the story of a family whose heart beats to the rhythm of hooves and a love for everything equine is almost part of their genetic make-up. In the history of horseracing in India, there hasn't been any other family that has produced so many accomplished jockeys and horse lovers. Being a jockey was almost a family trade of the Alfords for four generations, and they have won every race worth winning and many more for years and years.

But before we proceed with the story, we need to understand what it means to be a jockey. It's a life of strict regimens. A jockey will typically start working at the age of sixteen, after having undergone some sort of informal training. The one thing he needs to keep an eye out for always is his weight (heavyweight jockeys weigh up to 55 kg, and lightweight jockeys about 45 kg). His daily routine rarely varies. He awakes at 4 a.m. and reaches the tracks by 4.30 a.m., where he exercises the horses for a good three hours. After a light breakfast of tea and toast, he visits the stables of his trainer. On the racetrack, he has to constantly negotiate the threats of taking a fall, or getting trampled on. Injuries sustained here have put premature ends to many careers.

This chronicle of the Alford family was told to me by Ruth Crizzle (nee Alford) with many useful additions from her brothers and nephews.

The narrative begins with William John Alford, who was born in 1866 in Victoria, Australia. He came to India in 1890 and settled and married Celina Dalrymple Scotjohnson, in Chennai. His life as a jockey began there. Later, he moved to Kolkata where he started a farm at Hastings. He imported Jersey cows from Australia and supplied dairy products to the army lodged at Fort William. He died in a fatal accident while driving a trap. The love for horses as a profession was passed on to his sons. The star of this generation of Alfords was Rutherford (Ford) Dalrymple Alford.

Ford became a jockey at the age of sixteen. He rode in all the major races from Meerut, Lucknow, Delhi and Karachi to Sri Lanka, Rangoon, Kolkata and Mumbai. He retired from riding at the age of fifty and did what many jockeys do after retiring—turned to training.

Ford had five sons: Ivan, Freddie, Richard, Ernest and Philip. He also had two daughters—Ruth and Gloria.

In 1964, the family moved to Kolkata from Lucknow and Delhi.

Richard Alford, one of Ford's sons, has had a most illustrious career in racing. In 1962, he began as an apprentice to Tom Alford, his uncle. He turned professional at the age of sixteen. His career since then has seen one amazing accomplishment after another. He has over 960 career wins. He used to ride for Maharani Gina Narayan. The horse which brought him the most laurels was Midnight Cowboy and he rode it to win the Derby and the Invitation Cup in Kolkata in 1975.

Richard also recorded wins in major Classics events. The Classics are the very acme of professional racing. He also had the distinction of being champion jockey at the Royal Calcutta Turf Club (RCTC) for six consecutive years.

After retiring as a jockey, he turned trainer, and his horses have done exceedingly well on the racetrack. As a trainer, he has worked for Sheikh Rashid Bourley of Kuwait and legendary owners like Dr M.A.M. Ramaswamy, winning major races for them, too.

Richard's son's, Rutherford Alford's, is a heartbreaking yet inspiring story.

He first rode a horse at the age of ten, and became an apprentice jockey at the age of thirteen. Rutherford's major wins included the Calcutta Colt's Trials. In 2003, he won the Kakatiya Cup in Hyderabad and the Bangalore Cup in 2006.

Unfortunately, Rutherford fell from a horse soon after this, and was disabled for life. Though confined to a wheelchair, he refused to give up on his love for racing, and became a trainer. He trains from a wheelchair now, and his first win was from a horse named Lycia Falcon in the Calcutta Million.

Richard's brothers, Ernest and Philip, also had their share of success. Ernest rode with distinction in Mumbai, and Philip had his share of winning moments in Kolkata. Philip now trains apprentices in the racing school at Hyderabad and is an experienced starter at the Kolkata racecourse. Unbelievable as it may sound, four Alford brothers once competed in the same race. What a finish it made for! They came in first, second, third and fourth.

Today, Christopher, Freddie Alford's son, continues the family tradition.

If careers are judged by wins and that too Classics wins, then Christopher is really a champion among champions. His wins, as of September 2012, was a staggering 1161. As I write this, he is still notching up wins in India.

Born in 1976, he started riding in 1994. His first ride was on a horse called All Star, and his first win was on Champagne Times. He has been declared the champion jockey of the RCTC seven times in succession.

Sadly, the great Alford tradition of professional jockeys is slowly drawing to a close. Many of the current generation of Alfords are ladies, and while women have worked as jockeys in other parts of the world, in India it is still not a preferred profession. None of the Alford women became a professional jockey, though their love for horses, and the support they provided their sons, husbands and brothers was invaluable. Today, many in the family have taken to more traditional professions like airline hospitality, business executives and chefs. None of these has the short shelf-life of a jockey, who usually retires in his forties.

The Anglo-Indian community has produced some illustrious jockeys, pre-eminent among them being Robin Corner, Noel Remedios, Richard Alford, Ronnie Buttfoy and Nelson Reuben. Between them they have won thousands of races on every racetrack across the nation. It would be appropriate to mention that the community has also contributed a number of remarkable trainers to the world of horseracing, including Jack Goswell, Teddy McGaffin, Cliff Archer, Paddy Rylands, Charlie Elliott, Captain Fownes (trainer of Midnight Cowboy), his brother Major Fownes, and his nephew Lawrence Fownes.

The contribution of the remarkable Alford family, in particular, to Indian racing history is an astonishing story of dedication, talent and courage.

—ANDREW SCOLT

THE STORYTELLER

Irwin Allan Sealy (1951–)

Allan Sealy spent his early life in various towns in north India, as his father, Irwin Sealy, was a police officer in Uttar Pradesh. Irwin Sealy began his career as a police sergeant and retired as a Deputy Superintendent. Allan Sealy's mother was a teacher who taught dance in schools in the many little towns to which her husband was posted.

From his father, Sealy learnt the important lesson of self-reliance—how to repair furniture, plumbing, repairing gadgets, and other such useful skills. His mother passed on her culinary talents to him. She left him over a hundred recipes which he has preserved carefully over the years.

Both Allan and his elder sister, Janet, studied at La Martiniere, Lucknow. At school and college, gymnastics was Allan's favourite activity and he made it to the college team. Singing and painting were his obsessions. Both played a significant part in his career. Music helped pay his passage to the US for higher studies, and colours have appeared over and over again in his writings.

The city of Lucknow became his hometown by default because his family never remained long enough in other towns. He has happy memories of life in the small towns of Uttar Pradesh—they made him what he says he remains to this day, a provincial unmoved by the sophists of the metropolis. It was to Lucknow that he returned to write his first novel, *Trotter-Nama,* a story set in the fictional city of Naqlau.

His studies took him out of the secluded world of small towns and he first went to St Stephen's College, New Delhi, where he studied English Literature. Here, he discovered his love for books and for research. He also found he had a talent for the stage and was involved in a variety of dramatic productions, from Shakespeare to Brecht. In his final year he was selected as the annual exchange student to the Honours College at Western Michigan University, USA.

While in Delhi, he formed a singing duo with his classmate Chris Lugg, and was invited to sing over the summer of 1971 at Trincas, in Kolkata. The owners of Trincas, Josh and Puri, looked after them well and he earned enough to pay half his fare to America.

Life in an American college brought about more changes in perceptions and helped further shape his literary aspirations. Looking to study the literature of the former colonies (what was called Commonwealth Literature) he went to Canada and discovered a range of literatures and authors he had been unaware of till then. He wrote his doctorate on the Guyanese writer, Wilson Harris.

After his Master's degree, Sealy crossed continents and arrived in Australia, where he worked at the University of Sydney. His parents had decided to migrate to Australia but for Sealy, India remained home, and he settled in Dehra Dun. They bought a piece of land and built the house where he and his wife, a New Zealander, now live downhill from another great Anglo-Indian author, Ruskin Bond. They have a daughter, Deepa Rosa.

Allan Sealy is today recognized as one of India's foremost writers in the English language. His works show an astonishing range and versatility—from a magnum opus in the epic tradition, to a story about the film industry, to travelogues, to life in the mountains—his works surprise and entertain in equal measure. He was awarded the Padma Shri in 2012.

His first novel took seven years in the making. He had been reading widely about India and would smart from time to time at the representation of Anglo-Indians in books both by Indians and the British. After reading John Master's *Bhowani Junction* he decided it was time to redress old injuries. Apart from settling scores, he was also keen to write an informative account of Anglo-Indians which would not be a straight history. For years he travelled around the world gathering information from sources, primary and secondary.

Then, when he was ready to begin, he happened to be reading Abul Fazl's *Akbar-nama* and suddenly found his form. It was a form of the long epic novel that allowed him to 'bung all the material he had gathered into one big sack and give it a good shake'. The *Trotter-Nama*, published in 1988, is a mock epic that is a chronicle of seven generations of an Anglo-Indian family, a linking together of fictional but also historical figures to produce an insider's account. The novel was an amazing first work of fiction and established

Sealy's name as a rising star in the literary world. He won the Sahitya Akademi Prize and the Commonwealth Writer's Award for *Trotter-Nama*.

After *Trotter-Nama* he wrote a satire called *Hero*. It was written like a movie script with an interval in the middle for chips and ice-cream, set in Mumbai and Delhi.

One outstanding work followed another. *From Yukon to Yucatan* was the account of a North American journey. *The Everest Hotel* was set in the Doon Valley, and its mood was quiet and contemplative. It won the first Crossword Award in 1998.

The Brainfever Bird was set in Delhi, or the walled city of Shahjahanabad. This area, whose gullies he still explores when he can, had fascinated Sealy since his college days. The novel is a kind of a thriller, with a Russian element that came out of his readings of Russian literature and a visit to Moscow and St Petersburg.

And colours, which have dominated his vision of life, took centrestage in *Red*. 'Colour is part of the whole of writing,' he said.

At present, Allan Sealy is working on a non-fiction narrative that started out as the stories of two men, his *mali* and his *mistri*. His narrative has swelled to take in all the people who have at one time or another worked on the 433 square yards where he and his wife now live. It is a natural and social history of his surroundings which takes the form of an almanac. The book is a worm's eye view of history, far removed from grand narratives, and presents the extraordinary through the life stories of common men and women, people who actually populate our daily lives.

The sensitivity, breadth of knowledge and fine literary

sense that Sealy brings to each of his works will preserve his name as one among the greats of Indian writers in English.

—ERROL O'BRIEN

A CRICKETER AND A GENTLEMAN—ROGER TO THAT!

Roger Michael Humphrey Binny (1955–)

Roger Michael Humphrey Binny: you can't get a more Anglo-Indian name than that!

From the mid-eighties to mid-nineties, I was working as a sports journalist in India. At the time, I had a few encounters with this soft-spoken, almost shy sportsperson, the first Anglo-Indian to play international cricket for India.

During one such chat, I enquired how he got the name Humphrey. Usually, the third name for us Anglo-Indians is that of a Christian saint, and is bestowed on us at the church ceremony of Confirmation just prior to adolescence. I had never heard of a saint by the name 'Humphrey'. So I was surprised when Binny told me that there is indeed a St Humphrey, who was a Benedictine bishop of a small French town in 856 AD, and who fled the Norman invaders.

Roger is the only Anglo-Indian I know with Humphrey

as his third name. The other one that Roger obtained, and which was not as obscure as his Confirmation name, and neither did it relate to a Christian saint, was the nickname he was given on the cricket field—Jack, and variations such as Jacks/Jacko etc.

A common quiz question related to Indian cricket trivia is: how did Roger Binny get the nickname 'Jack'. The accepted answer is that it is derived from 'Jackfruit'—the shape of his bottom! Or so some female fans claimed, and now the quizmasters have come to accept this answer!

The story of this jackfruit shape also gave credence to another interesting piece of trivia: that his posterior was extra prominent as a result of his days training as a javelin thrower. It also apparently contributed to that unique and completely unorthodox posture during his bowling delivery when his back foot fell parallel rather than perpendicular to the bowling crease—a trick that baffled the batsman. Binny's action was much talked about during the 1983 World Cup, and was one of the factors that made him the highest wicket-taker in the tournament.

Despite his many sporting and other achievements, what stands out most about Roger Binny is the examples he has set as a human being for all Anglo-Indians, especially those living in India.

The first is his complete love for and loyalty to the country. And the second, the belief that even if one is a member of a small minority community like the Anglo-Indians, one can have a secure future in India by virtue of sheer hard work.

To put this into the Binny perspective, let me share this story of the time I spent with him in Bangalore, drinking a few beers at a club, and then going over to his home to meet his lovely family. This was after he had retired from cricket and had begun coaching in Bangalore while keeping his bank job.

It was obvious that despite the name and fame, this was a simple, down-to-earth, Anglo-Indian family where the Sunday lunch was a traditional family affair.

I brought up the topic of whether they had plans to migrate to Australia, where Binny's brother and other family had already moved.

While there was no definite answer that afternoon, it was clear to me that decision time was approaching: should they stay on and take it further in India, or break and move away and start from scratch, like so many of us have done after fleeing the nest.

Eventually, similar to my all-time sporting icon, Leslie Claudius, Binny and his family made a decision—and I daresay a well-thought one—to stay on and make the best of it in the country which he had given so much to and which had given him so much in return.

Like the great Claudius, who is so loved and revered in Kolkata, Binny has proved that his decision was a wise one. His resume even after retirement is an impressive one: coach of the Indian junior team which won the World Cup in 2000, Member of the Legislative Assembly in Karnataka, national selector, the list goes on and on.

Yet at the very top of that list it should say: a good, hardworking Indian, loyal to his country and community.

There is only one bone I have to pick with my friend Roger, and that is a very personal one.

When India won the right to co-host the 1996 Cricket World Cup, the Kolkata-based main sponsors asked my brothers and me for an idea to launch their sponsorship of the tournament. We suggested a first-ever reunification of the 1983 World Cup-winning team.

The project was ambitious, but we were determined to pull it off. It was just before I left India for Australia, and I pulled all the strings I could in Indian cricket, using the catchline in my phone calls and letters: 'farewell request before I go to Australia'.

What a memorable event it turned out to be! All the members of the winning team gathered in Kolkata, no questions asked, no fees involved. These were true champions of the country—the great Sunil Gavaskar, captain courageous Kapil Dev, the ever reliable Jimmy Amarnath, steady as a rock Dilip Vengsarkar, the flamboyant Kiri and Kris Srikanth, Yashpal Sharma, Madan Lal, Sandeep Patil, Balwinder Sandhu, Kirti Azad, Sunil Valson, everyone lined up on the stage side by side.

But not Roger Michael Humphrey Binny, my Anglo brethren!

Why? Well, Roger had a game that day. Not a cricket game, but in the sport he loves second best (I think!): golf.

That's the true Anglo in him. Forget the adoration and glamour; we will give up anything for a good game. So being a sports-crazy Anglo bloke myself, you are forgiven Roger, some seventeen years later.

And one last thing: Thank you for doing our community proud and showing so many younger Anglo-Indians that if they have the courage, the will, the determination, and if they put in the hard work, opportunities will come their way to make it good in the country of our birth.

We salute you, Roger!

—Clive Andrew Francis O'Brien (aka Andy O'Brien)

IMPOSSIBLE IS NOTHING
Derek O'Brien (1961–)

In 1892, Dadabhai Naoroji, a Parsi intellectual, became the first Indian to be elected to the British Parliament. After sixty-five years of Indian Independence, Derek O'Brien became the first Anglo-Indian to be elected to the Rajya Sabha of the Indian Parliament. I'm not trying to compare the two individuals, Naoroji and O'Brien, but to my mind, their elections deliver a similar message: 'Impossible is nothing'. Through Article 342 of the Indian Constitution, seats have always been reserved in the Lok Sabha and state assemblies for members of the Anglo-Indian community. But Derek has taken the longer, less travelled route to Parliament, by being elected to it. It is one for the Anglo-Indian 'Book of Firsts', and sends a message to all minority communities—that in today's India, an Anglo-Indian can take part effectively in mainstream Indian politics.

But for me, Derek was many other things first. When I leaf through the journals I have kept over the years, this entry from 13 March 1961 makes me smile:

> It is my twenty-first birthday and the entire world
> is my carefree stage. Isn't it wonderful to be young
> with so much to look forward to? And something
> else happened today that has brought our family so
> much joy. My cousin Neil took his wife Joyce to the
> Dufferin Nursing Home for the delivery of their first
> baby. Dr Cachatoor, a no-nonsense doughty Armenian
> lady, delivered a BABY BOY! I sent a few slices of my
> chocolate birthday cake to Joyce.

Here the entry ends, and memories begin.

A few weeks later, a cuddly ball of fluff was taken to the
Church of Christ the King in Park Circus. My sister Lorraine
and I were his godparents. The child was named Derek Peter.

Derek grew up in my grandmother Nellie O'Brien's house,
as we all did. His two brothers, Andy and Barry, arrived a
year apart each. My own three children, too, came into the
world a few years later, and the house was always filled with
the sounds of the children's laughter and banter.

Their companions were the neighbourhood Bengali
children with whom they played vociferous games of *gulli
danda* and street cricket. Festivals, both Hindu and Christian,
were celebrated by them with equal fervor. Derek and his
siblings picked up the choicest abuse, *gala gali*, with great
alacrity. But their great grandmother, the venerable Nellie,
also made sure that each of the children also learned refined
Bengali. For her, it was imperative that the younger generations
assimilate into the fabric of the society they were living in.

Derek showed an early aptitude for the languages, picking
up Bengali with ease and, like all the O'Brien children, spoke

a mix of Bengali and English at home. He was also a keen and confident elocutionist, winning many public speaking prizes at school and *para* competitions. For a short while, when their father was posted in Delhi with Oxford University Press, the whole family moved there. Derek studied at St Columba's School at the time, but the major part of his education was at St Xavier's Collegiate School in Kolkata and Scottish Church College, Kolkata.

Derek, like most Anglo-Indian boys, was sports crazy. He was a very good soccer and basketball player. This addiction to all forms of sports has stayed with him into his adult life. In the football field his position was between the goalposts. He went on to captain his school in both football and basketball. Later on, he was the goalkeeper for his club, the Dalhousie Institute, playing alongside a host of former India internationals.

His guru at the club was P. C. Wong, the Chinese-Indian goalie nicknamed the Great Wall of China. Opposing strikers could rarely score against Wong's spectacular abilities. Derek picked up many tricks of the trade from Wong and developed a sharp sense of anticipation. However, Derek had one handicap: he wore spectacles. These were held in place with a handkerchief or a band around his forehead when he played. But regardless of the threat of a broken wrist or shattered spectacles, he was an enthusiastic and skilled goalkeeper.

While he was still a second-year student at Scottish Church College, Derek started working part-time with *Sportsworld* magazine, setting their weekly sports crossword. From there he gradually moved to writing on sports at a time when the magazine was edited by the legendary Tiger Pataudi. When he finished his third year of college, he already had a year's experience of sports writing. Not one to be bogged down by academics, Derek did not sit for his final Honours examination, yet landed a job with the advertising firm of JWT. A year later, he moved to Ogilvy, Kolkata, where he stayed on for eight years and became the Creative Head.

Derek and his brothers had inherited a love for quizzing from their father. While he was working in journalism and advertising, Derek started conducting quizzes on the weekends. The vibrant quiz culture of the city now awoke the entrepreneur in him. Restless for new challenges and raring to explore new horizons, Derek decided to give up his job and plunge headlong into the world of quizzing. His announcement to the family in 1992, 'I'm going to become a professional quizmaster,' startled them, but they kept faith in his ability to handle challenges.

Big Ideas was formed that year, which later morphed into Derek O'Brien & Associates. From the dining table at home, this quizzing empire has reached corporate proportions. Today, it is a vibrant, young company of over seventy people, with an adroit research team, trained presenters and skilled production and school relationship-building associates to handle stage and television productions. The North Star Quiz sponsored by Bata was his very first annual, national venture. Next came the Bournvita Quiz Contest, which had been aired on radio for years, anchored by Hamid Sayani and later Ameen Sayani as quizmasters. In 1992, when the contest entered its television avatar, it was anchored by Derek O'Brien. Generations of children have participated in the show, making it one of India's longest-running television quiz shows, an instantly recognizable name, and no small part of the credit for this lies with the quizmaster, Derek.

Always seeking innovation, Derek is credited with having conducted the first quiz show on Twitter in 2010 (his Twitter handle @quizderek has a huge following). As quizmaster, Derek is known all over Asia, and along with his team of associates, conducts school and corporate quizzes both in India and outside.

In keeping with the company motto of 'Making knowledge interesting to help people grow', Derek also became a best-selling reference book author. He has written a number of successful general knowledge, quiz and school textbooks, published by the best publishers of the country.

In 2004, Derek realized that being just a corporate czar was not what he wanted from life, though his work revolved around his passion for quizzing. Determined to find a meaningful way in which he could contribute to the state he has loved and lived in, Bengal, Derek joined the All India Trinamool Congress, a political party with its base in West Bengal. He committed himself to the titanic struggle spearheaded by his leader Mamata Banerjee who appointed him spokesperson of the party. The year 2011 saw the Trinamool Congress sweep the Assembly polls with a landslide victory that ended thirty-four years of Communist rule in West Bengal.

Derek is currently the vice president of the party and a key member of its think tank. His ability to defend the party's policies and speak convincingly in the media along with his steadfast commitment to his party were two of the primary reasons he was elected on a Trinamool Congress ticket to Parliament. After being an MP for just one year Derek was elevated as Chief Whip of the party in the Rajya Sabha.

In October 2012, five Indian parliamentarians were chosen to represent the country at the United Nations. Among them was this rising star of Indian politics. On 22 October 2012, Derek O'Brien climbed another peak: he became the first

Anglo-Indian to address the UN General Assembly.

Derek married Rila Banerjee in 1991, and his daughter Aanya was born in 1995. He is now married to Dr Tonuca Basu, a doctor who lives and works in New York.

What makes Derek O'Brien tick, and what gives him the greatest pleasure from among the myriads of activities he is so closely and passionately involved with? I popped this question to Derek. He smiled and said, 'It comes from a humble acknowledgement of my failings, that I need to constantly work to make myself a better person. My family, my work, and Bengal define me, and I will keep doing what it takes to be worthy of them.'

—ERROL O'BRIEN

BEAUTY WITH A PURPOSE

Diana Hayden (1973–)

The year: 1997

Location: Seychelles islands, in the middle of the Indian Ocean.

Eric Morley, the founder of the Miss World Beauty Pageant takes the stage in the final moments.

In keeping with tradition, he announces:

'The Second Runner-up is Miss South Africa.

'The First Runner-Up is Miss New Zealand.

'And Miss World 1997... is Miss India!'

Diana Hayden walks up in a daze to be crowned, palms on her cheeks in disbelief. This is the moment that defines her, and the audience rises to its feet to give her a standing ovation.

Anglo-Indians, known for their proficiency in sports like hockey, billiards and cricket, have produced many champions. Twenty-four-year-old Hayden was the first Anglo-Indian to be adjudged 'The Most Beautiful Woman in the World'.

Hayden won an unprecedented foursome—Miss Photogenic, Miss Beachwear, Miss Asia/Oceanic Beauty Queen, Miss World—at this contest. Though she disliked the tag 'Beauty Queen', it was a term she came to accept.

Hayden was born in Hyderabad and schooled at St Ann's up to the eighth standard. She continued her education thereafter through the Open School and in correspondence courses.

As a child she was ever the tomboy. But her childhood was not an easy one. Her parents divorced when she was still quite young, and she had to start working in her early teens. Her large extended family, raucous and rambunctious, was however, a source of joy always. These early hardships and the difficulties contributed to her resilience and brought out the best in her.

With two hundred and fifty rupees in her purse Hayden moved to Mumbai in the early 1990s. She was taken in by a kindly couple who waived lodging rent till better days came for her. She found work as a receptionist, telephone operator and even a salesgirl at the Crawford Market. Finally, she moved on to working as an event manager in a company called Encore. She worked backstage and managed green rooms, supervising the wardrobe of artistes before their performances. From here she went on to work at BMG Crescendo where she assisted in managing the careers of singers Anaida and Mehnaz.

It was on Anaida's advice that she sent in her photographs for the Femina Miss India contest in 1997. She entered and won and was selected to represent the country in the Miss World contest to be held later in the year.

At the Miss India contest Hayden also won the Miss Beautiful Smile title. Though she missed out on winning the Miss Beautiful Hair crown, after winning the Miss World title,

L'Oreal signed her on as a brand ambassador for its hair products.

Hayden now feels contestants need to be themselves at these contests. Too much emphasis is paid now on the externals—the costumes and the make-up—and the girls have become more models than people with beauty and purpose. 'There is too much grooming and they create clones within one month of rehearsing. This is where contestants are going wrong,' she says.

In 1997, Hayden, elegantly dressed in white, said at the contest, 'I draw inspiration from a famous writer and poet, William Butler Yeats, who wrote "In dreams begin responsibility". Well, for me this title is that dream and the responsibility it brings I cherish that in some small way I can make a difference and help the dreams of others.'

As winner of Miss World, Hayden received a prize award of $100,000. She was required to make fifty appearances to promote the Seychelles as a tourist spot. True to her dream, she also helped to raise millions of dollars for charities in her capacity as Miss World. She was the ambassador for Child Relief and You and for Child and Police, a rehabilitation project under the Dr Reddy Foundation, Hyderabad. Hayden remains passionate about charity work and is also involved in the activities of the Spastics Society of India.

Following her tenure with the Miss World Organization, she moved to the UK and studied acting at the Royal Academy of Dramatic Arts, London. She also studied at the Drama Studio, London, where she concentrated on the works of Shakespeare and earned a Best Actress nomination of the studio.

In 2001, she made her screen debut in the film version of Shakespeare's *Othello* in South Africa. On returning to India she played a small role in the Bollywood film, *Tehzeeb* in 2003, and had a bigger part in *Ab…Bas* in 2004. *A Loving Doll*, a supernatural thriller, is the next film starring her.

In 2005, the History Channel approached Diana to host a three-month series called *Biography with Diana Hayden* where in addition to featuring prominent world leaders, Hollywood actors and sports champions, she had a series of interviews with Indian celebrity guests.

It was the first time that the History Channel had signed an Indian host for a show, and it went on to become one of the most successful programmes of the year for the channel.

After many busy years working in the media, at live shows and fashion shows, Hayden decided to take time off to write a book. It took her two and a half years of working in seclusion to complete it. Called *A Beautiful Truth,* she has done the illustrations and design herself. The book contains everything on the 'art of grooming for women'. There is no advocating of brand names but it sets out to help women of all ages with beauty and grooming tips.

'I have helped groom girls and boys for pageants and as airline personnel. All the information is contained in this book. It is something that emerged from my lectures. My work covers everything from how to determine your body shape and skin type, to how to dress accordingly and how to conduct yourself. I have tried to make the book humorous and readable, with anecdotes from my life like the instances when I made an ass of myself. It is the biggest thing that I have done since Miss World,' Hayden said on the release of the book in 2012.

With so many accomplishments behind her, Hayden is not one to rest. Brimming with ideas and plans, this Anglo-Indian beauty will continue to light up our lives with her beauty and kindness for years.

—ERROL O'BRIEN

NOTES ON CONTRIBUTORS

Andrew Scolt is an Anglo-Indian who lives in Kolkata. He was the Associate Editor of *Telegraph in Schools*, a weekly newspaper for students, for four years. He has over ten years of experience as a quizmaster, having conducted over 1,000 shows across India. He has also hosted quiz shows in Pakistan, Kathmandu, Singapore and the Middle East. He has been a key member of Derek O'Brien & Associates for the past six years.

Andy O'Brien is an Anglo-Indian born and educated in Kolkata, where he was based as an award-winning international sports journalist with *Sportsworld* magazine from the 1980s to the mid 1990s, before he migrated to Australia. He lives in Perth with his Kolkata-born Anglo-Indian wife and his two Australia-born sons, and visits India regularly to catch up with family and friends, and 'to show his sons their roots and heritage'.

Ashok Malik has been a journalist for over twenty years and his columns appear in several Indian and international publications. As an old Calcuttan, he knows Neil O'Brien for longer than he can remember. As an old quizzer, he has lost to Neil O'Brien more often than he would want to remember.

Derek O'Brien was born in Kolkata. He started his career as a journalist, and then worked as an advertising professional before following his greatest passion—quizzing. Today, he is one of Asia's most well-known quizmasters and has conducted numerous television and live shows. He is also CEO of Derek O'Brien & Associates. In 2004, he joined active politics when he became a member of the Trinamool Congress. In 2011, he was elected to the Rajya Sabha as a Member of Parliament.

Peter Moore was born in Kolkata and educated at St Xavier's College. He worked for the Kolkata Police for a number of years before moving to Australia.

Ronald Forbes lives in Canada with his wife, Patricia, who is Percy Carroll's daughter. Percy Carroll had five other children, Arthur and Diana (Foran) who live in England; Maureen (Lobo) who lives in India; Lita (Robertson) who lives in Australia; and Brian who lives in India.

Ruskin Bond has been writing for over sixty years, and has now over 120 titles in print—novels, collections of stories, poetry, essays, anthologies, and books for children. His first novel, *The Room on the Roof*, received the prestigious John Llewellyn Rhys award in 1957. He has also received the Padma Shri, and two awards from the Sahitya Akademi—one for his short stories and another for his writings for children. In 2012, the Delhi government gave him its Lifetime Achievement award. Born in 1934, Ruskin Bond grew up in Jamnagar, Shimla, New Delhi and Dehra Dun. Apart from three years in the UK, he has spent all his life in India, and now lives in Mussoorie with his adopted family.

Soutik Biswas was a Reuters Fellow at the University of Oxford. He has worked with Indian newspapers and magazines and at an international newspaper as a correspondent and an editor before joining the BBC. He has covered elections in Afghanistan and Sri Lanka, the tsunami in India and Sri Lanka, and militancy in Kashmir.

ACKNOWLEDGEMENTS

The editor would like to acknowledge the following for their contributions to this book:

- Andrew Scolt for writing the articles on Helen Richardson and the Alfords.
- Andy O'Brien for writing the article on Roger Binny.
- Ashok Malik for writing the article on Neil O'Brien.
- Derek O'Brien for writing the article on Nellie Bella O'Brien.
- Peter Moore for writing the article on Ronnie Moore.
- Ronald Forbes for permission to reprint his article on Percy Carroll.
- Ruskin Bond for permission to reprint his essay 'The Writer on the Hill'.
- Soutik Biswas for permission to reprint his article on Garney Nyss.

I would also like to thank the family members of some of

the personalities featured here for speaking to me and sharing their memories and thoughts with me.

Thank you to Sudeshna Shome Ghosh for editing the book with interest and care; and Mahua Basu of Derek O'Brien & Associates for working with me on this project.

The article on James Skinner was written after consulting a paper put together by Sumit Walia and published in *Bharat Rakshak* and articles published in the *Hindu*.

This book has been written to commemorate the International Anglo-Indian Reunion, 2013. It has also been written to assist projects set up by the Calcutta Anglo-Indian Service Society.